IRISH SHORT STORIES
Vol I

IRISH
SHORT STORIES
VOL I

Selected and introduced by
David Marcus

NEW ENGLISH LIBRARY

First published in Great Britain in 1980 in one volume by
The Bodley Head Ltd as *The Bodley Head Book of Irish Short Stories*

First NEL Paperback Edition in two volumes April 1982

NEL Books are published by
New English Library,
Barnard's Inn, Holborn,
London EC1N 2JR, a division of Hodder and Stoughton Ltd.

Typeset by Fleet Graphics, Enfield, Middlesex.

Made and printed in Great Britain by Cox and Wyman,
Reading

British Library C.I.P.

Irish Short Stories.

1
1. Short stories, English—Irish authors
2. English fiction—20th century
I. Marcus, David
823'.01'0809415[FS]   PR8875

ISBN 0-450-05378-4

Contents

Thanks are due to the following copyright-holders for
permission to reprint the stories listed:

'A Day in the Dark' by Elizabeth Bowen (Curtis Brown Ltd); 'At
Night All Cats Are Grey' by Patrick Boyle (the author); 'Joy' by
Daniel Corkery (Executor of the Estate of the late Daniel
Corkery); 'St Patrick's Day in the Morning' by Lynn Doyle (Mrs
Wyn Fisher and Duckworth Ltd); 'The Sisters' by James Joyce
(the Society of Authors as the literary representatives of the
Estate of James Joyce, the Executors of the Estate of James Joyce
and Jonathan Cape Ltd); 'Happiness' by Mary Lavin (the author
and Constable & Co. Ltd); 'The Ring' by Bryan MacMahon (the
author); 'The White Mare' by Michael McLaverty (the author
and Poolbeg Press Ltd); 'A Letter to Rome' by George Moore
(J.C. Medley and Colin Smythe Ltd); 'The Babes in the Wood' by
Frank O'Connor (Hamish Hamilton Ltd and A.D. Peters & Co.
Ltd); 'The Kitchen' by Sean O'Faolain (the author and Jonathan
Cape Ltd); 'The Landing' by Liam O'Flaherty (the author and
Jonathan Cape Ltd); 'Trinket's Colt' by E. Œ Somerville and
Martin Ross (John Farquharson Ltd); 'Desire' by James
Stephens (the Society of Authors as the literary representatives of
the Estate of James Stephens); 'Not Isaac' by Anthony C. West
(the author).

Introduction
to the Collection

The modern Irish short story is about as old as the century, that is, as old as the modern short story itself. Literary historians generally regard Gogol and Hawthorne as the fathers, respectively, of the short story in Russia and America (the other two countries reckoned to have been the major developers of the *genre*) yet the modern Irish short story is very seldom credited with significant parentage. But in fact it was not the immaculate conception it might appear to have been, with giants such as Liam O'Flaherty and James Joyce materialising as if by some form of literary abiogenesis: it had not only a father, but a mother as well. The father was George Moore (and it is perhaps characteristic of that smooth-tongued charmer that he was himself the first to claim fatherhood – what's more, to claim it long before there was any child on the way); the mother was (were?) that remarkable writing team of Edith Somerville and Martin Ross.

No literary parentage could have been more fruitful of promise, for father and mother emerged from the two widely-opposed cultures (Catholic and native/Protestant, or Anglo, and settler) which had become the constituents of the Irish family. Their attitude to the Irish society of their time – indeed the very areas of their concern – could not have been more divergent, but just as many of the latter's antecedents had taken on the ways and customs of the native and become 'more Irish than the Irish themselves', so did their literary descendants gradually come to write 'Irish' stories which were as germane and as committed as those being produced by the descendants of the former. Time had written off the condescensions and antagonisms, and whereas in seven centuries of history the political transplant had not yet successfully taken, in less than a single century the literary transplant was complete and both host and guest were part of the one native tradition.

The Irish pre-eminence in the field of the short story has

frequently been remarked upon by commentators, both native and foreign. But what accounts for such pre-eminence? How is it that a country which boasts no notable tradition of novel-writing repeatedly throws up outstanding short story writers? The explanation can, I believe, be traced to the fortuitous correspondence between two prominent Irish characteristics and the two vital ingredients of the short story.

Words are to the writer's art much as bricks are to a house, and just as a house is not a home, a way with words will not, alone and of itself, be sufficient equipment for a short story writer. It isn't even his primary equipment. The short story writer's basic and essential gift must be his approach to the material of life, his vision of the world about him, the outlook that is exclusive to him alone by virtue of his particular emotional and intellectual chemistry; in other words, his way of seeing; if his way of seeing is sufficiently individual, sufficiently differentiated, and if to it is added a gift of expression both above average and out of the ordinary, then you have a short story writer. A way of saying and a way of seeing are the flesh and spirit of the short story.

As far as a way of saying is concerned, there is general acknowledgement of the Irish writer's – indeed the Irishman's – exceptional facility. More often that not it is phraseology that has been the Irish short story's hallmark – a phraseology heady with colour and freshness, heady, above all, with an almost intoxicated sense of release. So persuasive has been the Irish way with words that the English language officially recognised it with a word of its own (suggested by the Irish of course): blarney.

What can account for the phenomenon of Irish-English? Why is it that, as H.E. Bates put it in his book *The Modern Short Story,* 'Ireland (and America) are now the places where the English language, both spoken and written, shows its most vigorous and most plastic vitality'? It is not difficult to explain the fecundity of American-English – a country the size of the U.S.A., in which so much regional variation is fuelled by such a hyper-competitive ethic, is bound to find its way of speech constantly energised by the cross-fertilisation of its society and the need to keep abreast of that society's mania for experimentation and invention. But the rhythms and scale of the Irish way of life are so different from those of America that such influences can hardly have contributed to the vigour and plasticity of Irish-English. What, however, must in large measure account for it is the fact that, as an American commentator, Charles E. May, wrote in

Short Story Theories, '. . . in Ireland the English language is not yet stale'. It is not stale because it was not until well into the nineteenth century that the English language in Ireland could be said to have been the only spoken language of the vast majority of the people. Before 1800 Irish held sway, and so when, during the ensuing hundred years, the native population adopted English as their vernacular, they were still thinking in Irish and consequently cobbled together their version of English with distinctively Irish words, inflections and constructions. And not only was the very shape and design of their English sentence influenced, but its style and personality – its air – was determined by what I can only call the philological impetus of the Irish language. This impetus is a direct reflection of the speaker's culture and way of life: in America, for instance, it is verbal (in the sense of being powered by verbs) because American-English has to keep pace with the go-ahead-and-get-things-done drive which its people have inherited from their pioneering stock; but in Ireland a traditionally near-to-standstill pace has afforded generous opportunity for the bodying forth of a bubbling Celtic imagination, and as a result simple conversation has been inflated to the status of a performance whose descriptive force has depended on its supply of adjectival lift-off. Yet this adjectival impetus is only the beginning of the Irish language's motive power: whereas in English the use of the adjective has to be restrained because it is normally placed before the noun and the noun has to be identified fairly smartly if the sense is not to be lost, in Irish the noun is placed first and so, the substantive being firmly established, there is almost no end to the number of adjectives which may be piled on it, each one adding more and more life and colour to the description. This particular adjectival balance of the Irish language would seem to me to be the major influence on the development of the English spoken in Ireland and written by Irish writers.

But what about the other – and more important – attribute of the short story writer, his special way of seeing? Is there a special Irish way of seeing? I would answer that question with the following anecdote.

Many years ago I was standing in a bus queue in the city of Cork. A station-wagon approached, its driver anxiously searching for a place to park. The area of roadway on either side of the bus-stop had, of course, to be kept clear, but there seemed to be just about a car's length free space between one of the white

11

boundary lines of that area and the row of cars parked beyond it. Into that space the station-wagon fitted itself and out of the vehicle stepped its driver – an ageing, genial, country gentleman type, all tweeds and twinkle – who immediately proceeded to inspect his position and assure himself that he had in fact found a space, however circumscribed, which would remove from him the fear of a fine for illegal parking. What he saw made him replace his smile of self-satisfaction with a puzzled frown: certainly his four wheels had cleared the white line, but the back of the station-wagon protruded over it and into the space allocated to the bus stop. A technical infringement, at the very least? Undecided, he turned to the bus queue, and, addressing no one in particular, asked 'Do you think I'd get away with that?' For a few minutes no one in particular hazarded an answer until an ancient, wizened, diminutive type took off his cap, slowly scratched his stubbled cheek, and replied, 'Well, sir, 'tis like this: are yeh lucky?'

For me that answer encapsulates some basic elements of the Irish way of seeing as well as the pith of their way of saying – the latter, of course, being in some part a product of the former. It has a touch of fatalism – inculcated into them by centuries of religious rigour and inclement weather; a large dash of super-stition – still rife in general customs and conventions, especially in rural areas; a hint of the accommodations sometimes made necessary with *force majeure* on the temporal plane – impressed upon them by the weight of their country's history; and of course the very form of the reply – a question answering a question – is the summation of the whole Irish temperament, the implicit belief that in this world, as in the world of the short story, there just are no answers; inklings and illuminations are the most one can expect.

Apart from the prowess of the Irish in the writing of short stories, there is the question of their addiction to the form. Why is the short story, rather than any other medium, the most popular Irish means of sophisticated artistic self-expression? Historical development suggests the answer. A peasant people intermit-tently at war – which for much of their history most of the Irish have been – is hardly likely to throw up significant painters, nor would their circumstances be conducive to the cultivation of a developing musical tradition (though in peasant peoples folk music usually flourishes and Irish folk songs are not only numerous but abound in ballads, i.e., short stories). This narrows

12

the field down to literature, and here the importance of the *seanachie* (storyteller) as a pivotal figure in rural Irish life down to the nineteenth century must account for the predisposition of the twentieth century Irish writer towards the short story.

Every anthologist has to don, with the best grace he can, some editorial harness – most particularly the anthology's title, which is his bit and bridle. In this case I have no problem deciding what qualifies as a short story, my standard being merely that of length rather than any academic distinction between tale, anecdote and short story proper. I have adopted 7,000 words as my upper limit – anything longer I regarded as having passed through the short story barrier into the area of the long short story – but the question 'What is an *Irish* short story?' cannot be answered by slide-rule or word count. The English critic, Walter Allen, in a recent series of articles on the Irish short story asked himself whether it was 'simply a story that happens·to be written in English by an Irishman'. Wise man, he didn't attempt to answer, though he did suggest that in its early days at least the Irish short story defined itself as being in general critical of the conditions of Irish life – Moore's *The Untilled Field* and Joyce's *Dubliners* being the trend-setters – and such a comment would be no less true of the Irish short story today.

I have not attempted to conform to any special pattern or to illustrate any particular trend in making the choice for this anthology and so I have arranged the stories in chronological order of author's birth. One rule, however, I felt, could not but be observed: every story had to have an Irish context. Apart from that my concern has been to present what in my opinion are out-standing and characteristic stories by as many as possible of the authors who have given the Irish short story its high reputation, as well as those of more recent and current times who are maintaining that reputation and shaping its future course.

David Marcus
Dublin, October 1980

GEORGE MOORE
A Letter to Rome

One morning the priest's housekeeper mentioned, as she gathered up the breakfast things, that Mike Mulhare had refused to let his daughter Catherine marry James Murdoch until he had earned the price of a pig.

'This is bad news,' said the priest, and he laid down the newspaper.

'And he waiting for her all the summer! Wasn't it in February last that he came out of the poor-hour? And the fine cabin he has built for her! He'll be so lonesome in it that he'll be going – '

'To America!' said the priest.

'Maybe it will be going back to the poor-house he'll be, for he'll never earn the price of his passage at the relief works.'

The priest looked at her for a moment as if he did not catch her meaning. A knock came at the door, and he said:

'The inspector is here, and there are people waiting for me.' And while he was distributing the clothes he had received from Manchester, he argued with the inspector as to the direction the new road should take; and when he came back from the relief works, his dinner was waiting. He was busy writing letters all the afternoon; and it was not until he had handed them to the post-mistress that he was free to go to poor James Murdoch, who had built a cabin at the end of one of the famine roads in a hollow out of the way of the wind.

From a long way off the priest could see him digging his patch of bog.

And when he caught sight of the priest he stuck his spade in the ground and came to meet him, almost as naked as an animal, bare feet protruding from ragged trousers; there was a shirt, but it was buttonless, and the breast-hair trembled in the wind – a likely creature to come out of the hovel behind him.

'It has been dry enough,' he said, 'all the summer; and I had a thought to make a drain. But 'tis hard luck, your reverence, and after building this house for her. There's a bit of smoke in the house now, but if I got Catherine I wouldn't be long making a chimney. I told Mike he should give Catherine a pig for her fortune, but he said he would give her a calf when I bought the pig, and I said, 'Haven't I built a fine house, and wouldn't it be a fine one to rear him in?'

And together they walked through the bog, James talking to the priest all the way, for it was seldom he had anyone to talk to.

'Now I mustn't take you any further from your digging.'

'Sure there's time enough,' said James. 'Amn't I there all day?'

'I'll go and see Mike Mulhare myself,' said the priest.

'Long life to your reverence.'

'And I will try to get you the price of the pig.'

'Ah, 'tis your reverence that's good to us.'

The priest stood looking after him, wondering if he would give up life as a bad job and go back to the poor-house; and while thinking of James Murdoch he became conscious that the time was coming for the priests to save Ireland. Catholic Ireland was passing away; in five-and-twenty years Ireland would be a Protestant country if – (he hardly dared to formulate the thought) – if the priests did not marry. The Greek priests had been allowed to retain their wives in order to avert a schism. Rome had always known how to adapt herself to circumstances; there was no doubt that if Rome knew Ireland's need of children she would consider the revocation of the decree of celibacy, and he returned home remembering that celibacy had only been made obligatory in Ireland in the twelfth century.

Ireland was becoming a Protestant country! He drank his tea mechanically, and it was a long time before he took up his knitting. But he could not knit, and laid the stocking aside. Of what good would his letter be? A letter from a poor parish priest asking that one of the most ancient decrees should be revoked! It would be thrown into the waste-paper basket. The cardinals are men whose thoughts move up and down certain narrow ways, clever men no doubt, but clever men are often the dupes of conventions. All men who live in the world accept the conventions as truths. It is only in the wilderness that the truth is revealed to man. 'I must write the letter! Instinct,' he said, 'is a surer guide than logic, and my letter to Rome was a sudden revelation.'

As he sat knitting by his own fireside his idea seemed to come out of the corners of the room. 'When you were at Rathowen,' his idea said, 'you heard the clergy lament that the people were

16

leaving the country. You heard the bishop and many eloquent men speak on the subject. Words, words, but on the bog road the remedy was revealed to you.

'That if each priest were to take a wife about four thousand children would be born within the year, forty thousand children would be added to the birthrate in ten years. Ireland can be saved by her priesthood!'

The truth of this estimate seemed beyond question, and yet, Father MacTurnan found it difficult to reconcile himself to the idea of a married clergy. 'One is always the dupe of prejudice,' he said to himself and went on thinking. 'The priests live in the best houses, eat the best food, wear the best clothes; they are indeed the flower of the nation, and would produce magnificent sons and daughters. And who could bring up their children according to the teaching of our holy church as well as priests?'

So did his idea unfold itself, and very soon he realised that other advantages would accrue, beyond the addition of forty thousand children to the birthrate, and one advantage that seemed to him to exceed the original advantage would be the nationalization of religion, the formation of an Irish Catholicism suited to the ideas and needs of the Irish people.

In the beginning of the century the Irish lost their language, in the middle of the century the characteristic aspects of their religion. It was Cardinal Cullen, who had denationalized religion in Ireland. But everyone recognised his mistake. How could a church be nationalised better than by the rescission of the decree of celibacy? The begetting of children would attach the priests to the soil of Ireland; and it could not be said that anyone loved his country who did not contribute to its maintenance. The priests leave Ireland on foreign missions, and every Catholic who leaves Ireland, he said, helps to bring about the very thing that Ireland has been struggling against for centuries – Protestantism.

His idea talked to him every evening, and, one evening, it said, 'Religion, like everything else, must be national,' and it led him to contrast cosmopolitanism with parochialism. 'Religion, like art, came out of parishes,' he said. He felt a great force to be behind him. He must write! He must write . . .

He dropped the ink over the table and over the paper, he jotted down his ideas in the first words that came to him until midnight; and when he slept his letter floated through his sleep.

'I must have a clear copy of it before I begin the Latin translation.'

He had written the English text thinking of the Latin that would come after, very conscious of the fact that he had written no Latin since he had left Maynooth, and that a bad translation would discredit his ideas in the eyes of the Pope's secretary, who was doubtless a great Latin scholar.

'The Irish priests have always been good Latinists,' he murmured, as he hunted through the dictionary.

The table was littered with books, for he had found it necessary to create a Latin atmosphere, and one morning he finished his translation and walked to the whitening window to rest his eyes before reading it over. But he was too tired to do any more, and he laid his manuscript on the table by his bedside.

'This is very poor Latin,' he said to himself some hours later, and the manuscript lay on the floor while he dressed. It was his servant who brought it to him when he had finished his breakfast, and, taking it from her, he looked at it again.

'It is as tasteless,' he said, 'as the gruel that poor James Murdoch is eating.' He picked up *St Augustine's Confessions*. 'Here is idiom,' he muttered, and he continued reading till he was interrupted by the wheels of a car stopping at his door. It was Meehan! None had written such good Latin at Maynooth as Meehan.

'My dear Meehan, this is indeed a pleasant surprise.'

'I thought I'd like to see you. I drove over. But – I am not disturbing you . . . You've taken to reading again. St Augustine! And you're writing in Latin!'

Father James' face grew red, and he took the manuscript out of his friend's hand.

'No, you mustn't look at that.'

And then the temptation to ask him to overlook certain passages made him change his mind.

'I was never much of a Latin scholar.'

'And you want me to overlook your Latin for you. But why are you writing Latin?'

'Because I am writing to the Pope. I was at first a little doubtful, but the more I thought of this letter the more necessary it seemed to me.'

'And what are you writing to the Pope about?'

'You see Ireland is going to become a Protestant country.'

'Is it?' said Father Meehan, and he listened, a little while. Then, interrupting his friend, he said:

'I've heard enough. Now, I strongly advise you not to send this

18

letter. We have known each other all our lives. Now, my dear MacTurnan – '

Father Michael talked eagerly, and Father MacTurnan sat listening. At last Father Meehan saw that his arguments were producing no effect, and he said:

'You don't agree with me.'

'It isn't that I don't agree with you. You have spoken admirably from your point of view, but our points of view are different.'

'Take your papers away, burn them!'

Then, thinking his words were harsh, he laid his hand on his friend's shoulder and said:

'My dear MacTurnan, I beg of you not to send this letter.'

Father James did not answer; the silence grew painful, and Father Michael asked Father James to show him the relief works that the Government had ordered.

But important as these words were, the letter to Rome seemed more important to Father Michael, and he said:

'My good friend, there isn't a girl that would marry us; now is there? There isn't a girl in Ireland who would touch us with a forty-foot pole. Would you have the Pope release the nuns from their vows?'

'I think exceptions should be made in favour of those in Orders. But I think it would be for the good of Ireland if the secular clergy were married.'

'That's not my point. My point is that even if the decree were rescinded we shouldn't be able to get wives. You've been living too long in the waste, my dear friend. You've lost yourself in dreams. We shouldn't get a penny. ''Why should we support that fellow and his family?'' is what they'd be saying.'

'We should be poor, no doubt,' said Father James. 'But not so poor as our parishioners. My parishioners eat yellow meal, and I eat eggs and live in a good house.'

'We are educated men, and should live in better houses than our parishioners.'

'The greatest saints lived in deserts.'

And so the argument went on until the time came to say good-bye, and then Father James said:

'I shall be glad if you will give me a lift on your car. I want to go to the post-office.'

'To post your letter?'

'The idea came to me – it came swiftly like a lightning-flash,

19

and I can't believe that it was an accident. If it had fallen into your mind with the suddenness that it fell into mine, you would believe that it was an inspiration.'

'It would take a good deal to make me believe I was inspired,' said Father Michael, and he watched Father James go into the post-office to register his letter.

At that hour a long string of peasants returning from their work went by. The last was Norah Flynn, and the priest blushed deeply for it was the first time he had looked on one of his parishioners in the light of a possible spouse; and he entered his house frightened; and when he looked round his parlour he asked himself if the day would come when he should see Norah Flynn sitting opposite to him in his armchair. His face flushed deeper when he looked towards the bedroom door, and he fell on his knees and prayed that God's will might be made known to him.

During the night he awoke many times, and the dream that had awakened him continued when he had left his bed, and he wandered round and round the room in the darkness, seeking a way. At last he reached the window and drew the curtain, and saw the dim dawn opening out over the bog.

'Thank God,' he said, 'it was only a dream – only a dream.'

And lying down he fell asleep, but immediately another dream as horrible as the first appeared, and his housekeeper heard him beating on the walls.

'Only a dream, only a dream,' he said.

He lay awake, not daring to sleep lest he might dream. And it was about seven o'clock when he heard his housekeeper telling him that the inspector had come to tell him they must decide what direction the new road should take. In the inspector's opinion it should run parallel with the old road. To continue the old road two miles further would involve extra labour; the people would have to go further to their work, and the stones would have to be drawn further. The priest held that the extra labour was of secondary importance. He said that to make two roads running parallel with each other would be a wanton humiliation to the people.

But the inspector could not appreciate the priest's arguments. He held that the people were thinking only how they might earn enough money to fill their bellies.

'I don't agree with you, I don't agree with you,' said the priest. 'Better go in the opposite direction and make a road to the sea.'

'You see, your reverence, the Government don't wish to engage

20

upon any work that will benefit any special class. These are my instructions.'

'A road to the sea will benefit no one . . . I see you are thinking of the landlord. But there isn't a harbour; no boat ever comes into that flat, waste sea.'

'Well, your reverence, one of these days a harbour may be made. An arch would look well in the middle of the bog, and the people wouldn't have to go far to their work.'

'No, no. A road to the sea will be quite useless; but its futility will not be apparent – at least, not so apparent – and the people's hearts won't be broken.'

The inspector seemed a little doubtful, but the priest assured him that the futility of the road would satisfy English ministers.

'And yet these English ministers,' the priest reflected, 'are not stupid men; they're merely men blinded by theory and prejudice, as all men are who live in the world. Their folly will be apparent to the next generation, and so on and so on for ever and ever, world without end.'

'And the worst of it,' the priest said, 'while the people are earning their living on these roads, their fields will be lying idle, and there will be no crops next year.'

'We can't help that,' the inspector answered, and Father MacTurnan began to think of the cardinals and the transaction of the business in the Vatican; cardinals and ministers alike are the dupes of convention. Only those who are estranged from habits and customs can think straightforwardly.

'If, instead of insisting on these absurd roads, the Government would give me the money, I'd be able to feed the people at a cost of about a penny a day, and they'd be able to sow their potatoes. And if only the cardinals would consider the rescission of the decree on its merits, Ireland would be saved from Protestantism.'

Some cardinal was preparing an answer – an answer might be even in the post. Rome might not think his letter worthy of an answer.

A few days afterwards the inspector called to show him a letter he had just received from the Board of Works. Father James had to go to Dublin, and in the excitement of these philanthropic activities the emigration question was forgotten. Six weeks must have gone by when the postman handed him a letter.

'This is a letter from Father Moran,' he said to the inspector who was with him at the time. 'The Bishop wishes to see me. We

21

will continue the conversation tomorrow. It is eight miles to Rathowen, and how much further is the Palace?'

'A good seven,' said the inspector. 'You're not going to walk it, your reverence?'

'Why not. In four hours I shall be there.' He looked at his boots first, and hoped they would hold together; and then he looked at the sky, and hoped it would not rain.

There was no likelihood of rain; no rain would fall today out of that soft dove-coloured sky full of sun, ravishing little breezes lifted the long heather, the rose-coloured hair of the knolls, and over the cut-away bog wild white cotton was blowing. Now and then a yellow-hammer rose out of the coarse grass and flew in front of the priest, and once a pair of grouse left the sunny hillside where they were nesting with a great whirr; they did not go far, but alighted in a hollow, and the priest could see their heads above the heather watching him.

'The moment I'm gone they'll return to their nests.'

He walked on, and when he had walked six miles he sat down and took a piece of bread out of his pocket. As he ate it his eyes wandered over the undulating bog, brown and rose, marked here and there by a black streak where the peasants had been cutting turf. The sky changed very little; it was still a pale, dove colour; now and then a little blue showed through the grey, and sometimes the light lessened; but a few minutes after the sunlight fluttered out of the sky again and dozed among the heather.

'I must be getting on,' he said, and he looked into the brown water, fearing he would find none other to slake his thirst. But just as he stooped he caught sight of a woman driving an ass who had come to the bog for turf, and she told him where he would find a spring, and he thought he had never drunk anything so sweet as this water.

'I've got a good long way to go yet,' he said, and he walked studying the lines of the mountains, thinking he could distinguish one hill from the other; and that in another mile or two he would be out of the bog. The road ascended, and on the other side there were a few pines. Some hundred yards further on there was a green sod. But the heather appeared again, and he had walked ten miles before he was clear of whins and heather.

As he walked he thought of his interview with the Bishop, and was nearly at the end of his journey when he stopped at a cabin to mend his shoe. And while the woman was looking for a needle and thread, he mopped his face with a great red handkerchief that

22

he kept in the pocket of his threadbare coat – a coat that had once been black, but had grown green with age and weather. He had outwalked himself and would not be able to answer the points that the Bishop would raise. The woman found him a scrap of leather, and it took him an hour to patch his shoe under the hawthorn tree.

He was still two miles from the Palace, and arrived footsore, covered with dust, and so tired that he could hardly rise from the chair to receive Father Moran when he came into the parlour.

'You seem to have walked a long way, Father MacTurnan.'

'I shall be all right presently. I suppose his Grace doesn't want to see me at once.'

'Well, that's just it. His Grace sent me to say he would see you at once. He expected you earlier.'

'I started the moment I received his Grace's letter. I suppose his Grace wishes to see me regarding my letter to Rome.'

The secretary hesitated, coughed, and went out, and Father MacTurnan wondered why Father Moran looked at him so intently. He returned in a few minutes, saying that his Grace was sorry that Father MacTurnan had had so long a walk, and he hoped he would rest awhile and partake of some refreshment . . . The servant brought in some wine and sandwiches, and the secretary returned in half an hour. His Grace was now ready to receive him . . .

Father Moran opened the library door, and Father MacTurnan saw the Bishop – a short, alert man, about fifty-five, with a sharp nose and grey eyes and bushy eyebrows. He popped about the room giving his secretary many orders, and Father MacTurnan wondered if the Bishop would ever finish talking to his secretary. He seemed to have finished, but a thought suddenly struck him, and he followed his secretary to the door, and Father MacTurnan began to fear that the Pope had not decided to place the Irish clergy on the same footing as the Greek. If he had, the Bishop's interest in these many various matters would have subsided: his mind would be engrossed by the larger issue.

As he returned from the door his Grace passed Father MacTurnan without speaking to him, and going to his writing-table he began to search amid his papers. At last Father MacTurnan said:

'Maybe your Grace is looking for my letter to Rome?'

'Yes,' said his Grace, 'do you see it?'

'It's under your Grace's hand, those blue papers.'

'Ah, yes,' and his Grace leaned back in his armchair, leaving

Father MacTurnan standing.

'Won't you sit down, Father MacTurnan?' he said casually. 'You've been writing to Rome, I see, advocating the revocation of the degree of celibacy. There's no doubt the emigration of Catholics is a very serious question. So far you have got the sympathy of Rome, and I may say of myself; but am I to understand that it was your fear for the religious safety of Ireland that prompted you to write this letter?'

'What other reason could there be?'

Nothing was said for a long while, and then the Bishop's meaning began to break in on his mind; his face flushed, and he grew confused.

'I hope your Grace doesn't think for a moment that – '

'I only want to know if there is anyone – if your eyes ever went in a certain direction, if your thoughts ever said, ''Well, if the decree were revoked – '' '

'No, your Grace, No. Celibacy has been no burden to me – far from it. Sometimes I feared that it was celibacy that attracted me to the priesthood. Celibacy was a gratification rather than a sacrifice.'

'I am glad,' said the Bishop, and he spoke slowly and emphatically, 'that this letter was prompted by such impersonal motives.'

'Surely, your Grace, His Holiness didn't suspect – '

The Bishop murmured an euphonious Italian name, and Father MacTurnan understood that he was speaking of one of the Pope's secretaries.

'More than once,' said Father MacTurnan, 'I feared if the decree were revoked, I shouldn't have had sufficient courage to comply with it.'

And then he told the Bishop how he had met Norah Flynn on the road. An amused expression stole into the Bishop's face, and his voice changed.

'I presume you do not contemplate making marriage obligatory; you do not contemplate the suspension of the faculties of those who do not take wives?'

'It seems to me that exception should be made in favour of those in Orders, and of course in favour of those who have reached a certain age like your Grace.'

The Bishop coughed, and pretended to look for some paper which he had mislaid.

'This was one of the many points that I discussed with Father Michael Meehan.'

'Oh, so you consulted Father Meehan,' the Bishop said, looking up.

'He came in the day I was reading over my Latin translation before posting it. I'm afraid the ideas that I submitted to the consideration of His Holiness have been degraded by my very poor Latin. I should have wished Father Meehan to overlook my Latin, but he refused. He begged of me not to send the letter.'

'Father Meehan,' said his Grace, 'is a great friend of yours. Yet nothing he could say could shake your resolution to write to Rome?'

'Nothing,' said Father MacTurnan. 'The call I received was too distinct and too clear for me to hesitate.'

'Tell me about this call.'

Father MacTurnan told the Bishop that the poor man had come out of the workhouse because he wanted to be married, and that Mike Mulhare would not give him his daughter until he had earned the price of a pig. 'And as I was talking to him I heard my conscience say, "No one can afford to marry in Ireland but the clergy." We all live better than our parishioners.'

And then, forgetting the Bishop, and talking as if he were alone with his God, he described how the conviction had taken possession of him – that Ireland would become a Protestant country if the Catholic emigration did not cease. And he told how this conviction had left him little peace until he had written his letter.

The priest talked on until he was interrupted by Father Moran.

'I have some business to transact with Father Moran now,' the Bishop said, 'but you must stay to dinner. You've walked a long way, and you are tired and hungry.'

'But, your Grace, if I don't start now, I shan't get home until nightfall.'

'A car will take you back, Father MacTurnan. I will see to that. I must have some exact information about your poor people. We must do something for them.'

Father MacTurnan and the Bishop were talking together when the car came to take Father MacTurnan home, and the Bishop said:

'Father MacTurnan, you have borne the loneliness of your parish a long while.'

'Loneliness is only a matter of habit. I think, your Grace, I'm better suited to the place than I am for any other. I don't wish to change, if your Grace is satisfied with me.'

'No one will look after the poor people better than yourself,

Father MacTurnan. But,' he said, 'it seems to me there is one thing we have forgotten. You haven't told me if you have succeeded in getting the money to buy the pig.'

Father MacTurnan grew very red . . . 'I had forgotten it. The relief works – '

'It's not too late. Here's five pounds, and this will buy him a pig.'

'It will indeed,' said the priest, 'it will buy him two!'

He had left the Palace without having asked the Bishop how his letter had been received at Rome, and he stopped the car, and was about to tell the driver to go back. But no matter, he would hear about his letter some other time. He was bringing happiness to two poor people, and he could not persuade himself to delay their happiness by one minute. He was not bringing one pig, but two pigs, and now Mike Mulhare would have to give him Catherine and a calf; and the priest remembered that James Murdoch had said – 'What a fine house this will be to rear them in.' There were many who thought that human beings and animals should not live together; but after all, what did it matter if they were happy? And the priest forgot his letter to Rome in the thought of the happiness he was bringing to two poor people. He could not see Mike Mulhare that night; but he drove down to the famine road, and he and the driver called till they awoke James Murdoch. The poor man came stumbling across the bog, and the priest told him the news.

E. ŒSOMERVILLE
AND MARTIN ROSS

Trinket's Colt

It was Petty Sessions day in Skebawn, a cold, grey day of February. A case of trespass had dragged its burden of cross summonses and cross swearing far into the afternoon, and when I left the bench my head was singing from the bellowings of the attorneys, and the smell of their clients was heavy upon my palate.

The streets still testified to the fact that it was market day, and I evaded with difficulty the sinuous course of carts full of soddenly screwed people, and steered an equally devious one for myself among the groups anchored round the doors of the public-houses. Skebawn possesses, among its legion of public-houses, one establishment which timorously, and almost imperceptibly, proffers tea to the thirsty. I turned in there, as was my custom on court days, and found the little dingy den, known as the Ladies' Coffee-room, in the occupancy of my friend Mr Florence McCarthy Knox, who was drinking strong tea and eating buns with serious simplicity. It was a first and quite unexpected glimpse of that domesticity that has now become a marked feature in his character.

'You're the very man I wanted to see,' I said as I sat down beside him at the oilcloth-covered table; 'a man I know in England who is not much of a judge of character has asked me to buy him a four-year-old down here, and as I should rather be stuck by a friend than a dealer, I wish you'd take over the job.'

Flurry poured himself out another cup of tea, and dropped three lumps of sugar into it in silence.

Finally he said, 'There isn't a four-year-old in this country that I'd be seen dead with at a pig fair.'

This was discouraging, from the premier authority on horse-flesh in the district.

'But it isn't six weeks since you told me you had the finest filly in your stables that was ever foaled in the County Cork,' I protested; 'what's wrong with her?'

'Oh, is it that filly?' said Mr Knox with a lenient smile; 'she's gone these three weeks from me. I swapped her and six pounds for a three-year-old Ironmonger colt, and after that I swapped the colt and nineteen pounds for that Bandon horse I rode last week at your place, and after that again I sold the Bandon horse for seventy-five pounds to old Welply, and I had to give him back a couple of sovereigns luck-money. You see I did pretty well with the filly after all.'

'Yes, yes – oh, rather,' I asserted, as one dizzily accepts the propositions of a bimetallist; 'and you don't know of anything else – ?'

The room in which we were seated was closely screened from the shop by a door with a muslin-covered window in it; several of the panes were broken, and at this juncture two voices that had for some time carried on a discussion forced themselves upon our attention.

'Begging your pardon for contradicting you, ma'am,' said the voice of Mrs McDonald, proprietress of the teashop, and a leading light in Skebawn Dissenting circles, shrilly tremulous with indignation, 'if the servants I recommend you won't stop with you, it's no fault of mine. If respectable young girls are set picking grass out of your gravel, in place of their proper work, certainly they will give warning!'

The voice that replied struck me as being a notable one, well-bred and imperious.

'When I take a barefooted slut out of a cabin, I don't expect her to dictate to me what her duties are!'

Flurry jerked up his chin in a noiseless laugh. 'It's my grandmother!' he whispered. 'I bet you Mrs McDonald don't get much change out of her!'

'If I set her to clean the pigsty I expect her to obey me,' continued the voice in accents that would have made me clean forty pigsties had she desired me to do so.

'Very well, Ma'am,' retorted Mrs McDonald, 'if that's the way you treat your servants, you needn't come here again looking for them. I consider your conduct is neither that of a lady nor a Christian!'

'Don't you, indeed?' replied Flurry's grandmother. 'Well, your opinion doesn't greatly distress me, for to tell you the truth, I don't think you're much of a judge.'

'Didn't I tell you she'd score?' murmured Flurry, who was by this time applying his eye to a hole in the muslin curtain. 'She's off,' he went on, returning to his tea. 'She's a great character! She's eighty-three if she's a day, and she's as sound on her legs as a three-year-old! Did you see that old shandrydan of hers in the street a while ago, and a fellow on the box with a red beard on him like Robinson Crusoe? That old mare that was on the near side – Trinket her name is – is mighty near clean bred. I can tell you her foals are worth a bit of money.'

I had heard of old Mrs Knox of Aussolas; indeed, I had seldom dined out in the neighbourhood without hearing some new story of her and her remarkable *ménage,* but it had not yet been my privilege to meet her.

'Well, now,' went on Flurry in his slow voice. 'I'll tell you a thing, that's just come into my head. My grandmother promised me a foal of Trinket's the day I was one-and-twenty, and that's five years ago, and deuce a one I've got from her yet. You never were at Aussolas? No, you were not. Well, I tell you the place there is like a circus with horses. She has a couple of score of them running wild in the woods, like deer.'

'Oh, come,' I said, 'I'm a bit of a liar myself – '

'Well, she has a dozen of them anyhow, rattling good colts too, some of them, but they might as well be donkeys, for all the good they are to me or any one. It's not once in three years she sells one and there she has them walking after her for bits of sugar, like a lot of dirty lapdogs,' ended Flurry with disgust.

'Well, what's your plan? Do you want me to make her a bid for one of the lapdogs?'

'I was thinking,' replied Flurry, with great deliberation, 'that my birthday's this week, and maybe I could work a four-year-old colt of Trinket's she has out of her in honour of the occasion.'

'And sell your grandmother's birthday present to me?'

'Just that, I suppose,' answered Flurry with a slow wink.

A few days afterwards a letter from Mr Knox informed me that he had 'squared the old lady, and it would be all right about the colt'. He further told me that Mrs Knox had been good enough to offer me, with him, a day's snipe shooting on the celebrated Aussolas bogs, and he proposed to drive me there the following Monday, if convenient. Most people found it convenient to shoot the Aussolas snipe bog when they got the chance. Eight o'clock on the following Monday morning saw Flurry, myself, and a groom packed into a dogcart, with portmanteaus, gun-cases, and two rampant red setters.

It was a long drive, twelve miles at least, and a very cold one. We passed through long tracts of pasture country, fraught, for Flurry, with memories of runs, which were recorded for me, fence by fence, in every one of which the biggest dog-fox in the country had gone to ground, with not two feet – measured accurately on the handle of the whip – between him and the leading hound; through bogs that imperceptibly melted into lakes, and finally down and down into a valley, where the fir-trees of Aussolas clustered darkly round a glittering lake, and all but hid the grey roofs and pointed gables of Aussolas Castle.

'There's a nice stretch of a demesne for you,' remarked Flurry, pointing downwards with the whip, 'and one little old woman holding it all in the heel of her fist. Well able to hold it she is, too, and always was, and she'll live twenty years yet, if it's only to spite the whole lot of us, and when all's said and done goodness knows how she'll leave it!'

'It strikes me you were lucky to keep her up to her promise about the colt,' I said.

Flurry administered a composing kick to the ceaseless striving of the red setters under the seat.

'I used to be rather a pet with her,' he said, after a pause; 'but mind you, I haven't got him yet, and if she gets any notion I want to sell him I'll never get him, so say nothing about the business to her.'

The tall gates of Aussolas shrieked on their hinges as they admitted us, and shut with a clang behind us, in the faces of an old mare and a couple of young horses, who, foiled in their break for the excitement of the outer world, turned and galloped defiantly on either side of us. Flurry's admirable cob hammered on, regardless of all things save his duty.

'He's the only one I have that I'd trust myself here with,' said his master, flicking him approvingly with the whip; 'there are plenty of people afraid to come here at all, and when my grand-mother goes out driving she has a boy on the box with a basket full of stones to peg at them. Talk of the dickens, here she is herself!'

A short, upright old woman was approaching, preceded by a white woolly dog with sore eyes and a bark like a tin trumpet; we both got out of the trap and advanced to meet the lady of the manor.

I may summarise her attire by saying that she looked as if she had robbed a scarecrow; her face was small and incongruously refined, the skinny hand that she extended to me had the grubby tan that bespoke the professional gardener, and was decorated with a magnificent diamond ring. On her head was a massive purple velvet bonnet.

'I am very glad to meet you, Major Yeates,' she said with an old-fashioned precision of utterance, 'your grandfather was a dancing partner of mine in old days at the Castle, when he was a handsome young aide-de-camp there, and I was – You may judge for yourself what I was.'

She ended with a startling little hoot of laughter, and I was aware that she quite realized the world's opinion of her, and was indifferent to it.

Our way to the bogs took us across Mrs Knox's home farm, and through a large field in which several young horses were grazing.

'There now, that's my fellow,' said Flurry, pointing to a fine-looking colt, 'the chestnut with the white diamond on his forehead. He'll run into three figures before he's done, but we'll not tell that to the old lady!'

The famous Aussolas bogs were as full of snipe as usual, and a good deal fuller of water than any bogs I had ever shot before. I was on my day, and Flurry was not, and as he is ordinarily an infinitely better snipe shot than I, I felt at peace with the world and all men as we walked back, wet through, at five o'clock.

The sunset had waned, and a big white moon was making the eastern tower of Aussolas look like a thing in a fairy tale or a play when we arrived at the hall door. An individual, whom I recognised as the Robinson Crusoe coachman, admitted us to a hall, the like of which one does not often see. The walls were panelled with dark oak up to the gallery that ran round three sides of it, the balusters of the wide staircase were heavily carved, and blackened portraits of Flurry's ancestors on the spindle side stared sourly down on their descendant as he tramped upstairs with the bog mould on his hobnailed boots.

We had just changed into dry clothes when Robinson Crusoe shoved his red beard round the corner of the door, with the information that the mistress said we were to stay for dinner. My heart sank. It was then barely half-past five. I said something about having no evening clothes and having to get home early.

'Sure the dinner'll be in another half hour,' said Robinson Crusoe, joining hospitably in the conversation, 'and as for evening clothes – God bless ye!'

The door closed behind him.

'Never mind,' said Flurry. 'I dare say you'll be glad enough to eat another dinner by the time you get home.' He laughed. 'Poor Slipper!' he added inconsequently, and only laughed again when I asked for an explanation.

Old Mrs Knox received us in the library, where she was seated by a roaring turf fire, which lit the room a good deal more effectively than the pair of candles that stood beside her in tall silver candlesticks. Ceaseless and implacable growls from under her chair indicated the presence of the woolly dog. She talked with confounding culture of the books that rose all round her to the ceiling; her evening dress was accomplished by means of an additional white shawl, rather dirtier than its congeners; as I took her in to dinner she quoted Virgil to me, and in the same breath screeched an objurgation at a being whose matted head rose suddenly into view from behind an ancient Chinese screen, as I have seen the head of a Zulu woman peer over a bush.

Dinner was as incongruous as everything else. Detestable soup in a splendid old silver tureen that was nearly as dark in hue as Robinson Crusoe's thumb, a perfect salmon, perfectly cooked, on a chipped kitchen dish; such cut glass as is not easy to find nowadays; sherry that, as Flurry subsequently remarked, would burn the shell off an egg; and a bottle of port, draped in immemorial cobwebs, wan with age, and probably priceless. Throughout the vicissitudes of the meal Mrs Knox's conversation flowed on undismayed, directed sometimes at me – she had installed me in the position of friend of her youth and talked to me as if I were my own grandfather – sometimes at Crusoe, with whom she had several heated arguments, and sometimes she would make a statement of remarkable frankness on the subject of her horse-farming affairs to Flurry, who, very much on his best behaviour, agreed with all she said, and risked no original remark. As I listened to them both, I remembered with infinite amusement how he had told me once that 'a pet name she had for him was "Tony Lumpkin", and no one but herself knew what she meant by it.' It seemed strange that she made no allusion to Trinket's colt or to Flurry's birthday, but, mindful of my instructions, I held my peace.

As, at about half-past eight, we drove away in the moonlight, Flurry congratulated me solemnly on my success with his grandmother. He was good enough to tell me that she would marry me to-morrow if I asked her, and he wished I would, even if it was

32

only to see what a nice grandson he'd be for me. A sympathetic giggle behind me told me that Michael, on the back seat, had heard and relished the jest.

We had left the gates of Aussolas about half a mile behind when, at the corner of a by-road, Flurry pulled up. A short squat figure arose from the black shadow of a furze bush and came out into the moonlight, swinging its arms like a cabman and cursing audibly.

'Oh murdher, oh murdher, Misther Flurry! What kept ye at all? 'Twould perish the crows to be waiting here the way I am these two hours – '

'Ah, shut your mouth, Slipper!' said Flurry, who, to my surprise, had turned back the rug and was taking off his driving coat, 'I couldn't help it. Come on, Yeates, we've got to get out here.'

'What for?' I asked, in not unnatural bewilderment.

'It's all right. I'll tell you as we go along,' replied my companion, who was already turning to follow Slipper up the by-road. 'Take the trap on, Michael, and wait at the River's Cross.' He waited for me to come up with him, and then put his hand on my arm. 'You see, Major, this is the way it is. My grandmother's given me that colt right enough, but if I waited for her to send him over to me I'd never see a hair of his tail. So I thought that as we were over here we might as well take him back with us, and maybe you'll give us a help with him; he'll not be altogether too handy for a first go off.'

I was staggered. An infant in arms could scarcely have failed to discern the fishiness of the transaction, and I begged Mr Knox not to put himself into this trouble on my account, as I had no doubt I could find a horse for my friend elsewhere. Mr Knox assured me that it was no trouble at all, quite the contrary, and that, since his grandmother had given him the colt, he saw no reason why he should not take him when he wanted him; also, that if I didn't want him he'd be glad enough to keep him himself; and finally, that I wasn't the chap to go back on a friend, but I was welcome to drive back to Shreelane with Michael this minute if I liked.

Of course I yielded in the end. I told Flurry I should lose my job over the business, and he said I could then marry his grandmother, and the discussion was abruptly closed by the necessity of following Slipper over a locked five-barred gate.

Our pioneer took us over about half a mile of country, knocking down stone gaps where practicable and scrambling over tall banks in the deceptive moonlight. We found ourselves at length in a field with a shed in one corner of it; in a dim group of farm buildings a little way off a light was shining.

'Wait here,' said Flurry to me in a whisper; 'the less noise the better. It's an open shed, and we'll just slip in and coax him out.'

Slipper unwound from his waist a halter, and my colleagues glided like spectres into the shadow of the shed, leaving me to meditate on my duties as Resident Magistrate, and on the questions that would be asked in the House by our local member when Slipper had given away the adventure in his cups.

In less than a minute three shadows emerged from the shed, where two had gone in. They had got the colt.

'He came out as quiet as a calf when he winded the sugar,' said Flurry; 'it was well for me I filled my pockets from grandmamma's sugar basin.'

He and Slipper had a rope from each side of the colt's head; they took him quickly across a field towards a gate. The colt stepped daintily between them over the moonlit grass; he snorted occasionally, but appeared on the whole amenable.

The trouble began later, and was due, as trouble often is, to the beguilements of a short cut. Against the maturer judgment of Slipper, Flurry insisted on following a route that he assured us he knew as well as his own pocket, and the consequence was that in about five minutes I found myself standing on top of a bank hanging on to a rope, on the other end of which the colt dangled and danced, while Flurry, with the other rope, lay prone in the ditch, and Slipped administered to the bewildered colt's hind quarters such chastisement as could be ventured on.

I have no space to narrate in detail the atrocious difficulties and disasters of the short cut. How the colt set to work to buck, and went away across the field, dragging the faithful Slipper, literally *ventre à terre,* after him, while I picked myself in ignominy out of a briar patch, and Flurry cursed himself black in the face. How we were attacked by ferocious cur dogs, and I lost my eye-glass; and how, as we neared the River's Cross, Flurry espied the police patrol on the road, and we all hid behind a rick of turf while I realised in fullness what an exceptional ass I was, to have been beguiled into an enterprise that involved hiding with Slipper from the Royal Irish Constabulary.

Let it suffice to say that Trinket's infernal offspring was finally handed over on the high road to Michael and Slipper, and Flurry drove me home in a state of mental and physical overthrow.

I saw nothing of my friend Mr Knox for the next couple of days, by the end of which time I had worked up a high polish on my misgivings, and had determined to tell him that under no circumstances would I have anything to say to his grandmother's birthday present. It was like my usual luck that, instead of writing a note to this effect, I thought it would be good for my liver to walk across the hills to Tory Cottage and tell Flurry so in person.

It was a bright, blustery morning, after a muggy day. The feeling of spring was in the air, the daffodils were already in bud, and crocuses showed purple in the grass on either side of the avenue. It was only a couple of miles to Tory Cottage by the way across the hills; I walked fast, and it was barely twelve o'clock when I saws its pink walls and clumps of evergreens below me. As I looked down at it the chiming of Flurry's hounds in the kennels came to me on the wind; I stood still to listen, and could almost have sworn that I was hearing again the clash of Magdalen bells, hard at work on May morning.

The path that I was following led downwards through a larch plantation to Flurry's back gate. Hot wafts from some hideous cauldron at the other side of a wall apprised me of the vicinity of the kennels and their cuisine, and the fir-trees round were hung with gruesome and unknown joints. I thanked heaven that I was not a master of hounds, and passed on as quickly as might be to the hall door.

I rang two or three times without response; then the door opened a couple of inches and was instantly slammed in my face. I heard the hurried paddling of bare feet on oil-cloth, and a voice, 'Hurry, Bridgie, hurry! There's quality at the door!'

Bridgie, holding a dirty cap on with one hand, presently arrived and informed me that she believed Mr Knox was out about the place. She seemed perturbed, and she cast scared glances down the drive while speaking to me.

I knew enough of Flurry's habits to shape a tolerably direct course for his whereabouts. He was, as I had expected, in the training paddock, a field behind the stable yard, in which he had put up practice jumps for his horses. It was a good-sized field with clumps of furze in it, and Flurry was standing near one of these with his hands in his pockets, singularly unoccupied. I supposed that he was prospecting for a place to put up another jump. He did not see me coming, and turned with a start as I spoke to him. There was a queer expression of mingled guilt and what I can only describe as divilment in his grey eyes as he greeted

35

me. In my dealings with Flurry Knox, I have since formed the habit of sitting tight, in a general way, when I see that expression.

'Well, who's coming next, I wonder!' he said, as he shook hands with me; 'it's not ten minutes since I had two of your d – d peelers here searching the whole place for my grandmother's colt!'

'What!' I exclaimed, feeling cold all down my back; 'do you mean the police have got hold of it?'

'They haven't got hold of the colt anyway,' said Flurry, looking sideways at me from under the peak of his cap, with the glint of the sun in his eye. 'I got word in time before they came.'

'What do you mean?' I demanded; 'where is he? For heaven's sake don't tell me you've sent the brute over to my place!'

'It's a good job for you I didn't,' replied Flurry, 'as the police are on their way to Shreelane this minute to consult you about it. *You*!' He gave utterance to one of his short diabolical fits of laughter. 'He's where they'll not find him, anyhow. Ho ho! It's the funniest hand I ever played!'

'Oh yes, it's devilish funny, I've no doubt,' I retorted, beginning to lose my temper, as is the manner of many people when they are frightened; 'but I give you fair warning that if Mrs Knox asks me any questions about it, I shall tell her the whole story.'

'All right,' responded Flurry; 'and when you do, don't forget to tell her how you flogged the colt out on to the road over her own bounds ditch.'

'Very well,' I said hotly, 'I may as well go home and send in my papers. They'll break me over this – '

'Ah, hold on, Major,' said Flurry soothingly, 'it'll be all right. No one knows anything. It's only on spec the old lady sent the bobbies here. If you'll keep quiet it'll all blow over.'

'I don't care,' I said, struggling hopelessly in the toils; 'if I meet your grandmother, and she asks me about it, I shall tell her all I know.'

'Please God you'll not meet her! After all, it's not once in a blue moon that she – ' began Flurry. Even as he said the words his face changed. 'Holy fly!' he ejaculated, 'isn't that her dog coming into the field? Look at her bonnet over the wall! Hide, hide for your life!' He caught me by the shoulder and shoved me down among the furze bushes before I realised what had happened.

'Get in there! I'll talk to her.'

I may as well confess that at the mere sight of Mrs Knox's

purple bonnet my heart had turned to water. In that moment I knew what it would be like to tell her how I, having eaten her salmon, and capped her quotations, and drunk her best port, had gone forth and helped to steal her horse. I abandoned my dignity, my sense of honour; I took the furze prickles to my breast and wallowed in them.

Mrs Knox had advanced with vengeful speed; already she was in high altercation with Flurry at no great distance from where I lay; varying sounds of battle reached me, and I gathered that Flurry was not – to put it mildly – shrinking from that economy of truth that the situation required.

'Is it that curby, long-backed brute? You promised him to me long ago, but I wouldn't be bothered with him!'

The old lady uttered a laugh of shrill decision. 'Is it likely I'd promise you my best colt. And still more, is it likely that you'd refuse him if I did?'

'Very well, ma'am.' Flurry's voice was admirably indignant. 'Then I suppose I'm a liar and a thief.'

'I'd be more obliged to you for the information if I hadn't known it before,' responded his grandmother with lightning speed; 'if you swore to me on a stack of Bibles you knew nothing about my colt I wouldn't believe you! I shall go straight to Major Yeates and ask his advice. I believe *him* to be a gentleman, in spite of the company he keeps!'

I writhed deeper into the furze bushes, and thereby discovered a sandy rabbit run, along which I crawled, with my cap well over my eyes, and the furze needles stabbing me through my stockings. The ground shelved a little, promising profounder concealment, but the bushes were very thick, and I laid hold of the bare stem of one to help my progress. It lifted out of the ground in my hand, revealing a freshly cut stump. Something snorted, not a yard away; I glared through the opening, and was confronted by the long, horrified face of Mrs Knox's colt, mysteriously on a level with my own.

Even without the white diamond on his forehead I should have divined the truth; but how in the name of wonder had Flurry persuaded him to couch like a woodcock in the heart of a furze brake? For a full minute I lay as still as death for fear of frightening him, while the voices of Flurry and his grandmother raged on alarmingly close to me. The colt, snorted, and blew long breaths through his wide nostrils, but he did not move. I crawled an inch or two nearer, and after a few seconds of cautious peering I grasped the position. They had buried him.

A small sandpit among the furze had been utilised as a grave; they had filled him in up to his withers with sand, and a few furze bushes, artistically disposed around the pit, have done the rest. As the depth of Flurry's guile was revealed, laughter came upon me lik a flood; I gurgled and shook apoplectically and the colt gazed at me with serious surprise, until a sudden outburst of barking close to my elbow administered a fresh shock to my tottering nerves.

Mrs Knox's woolly dog had tracked me into the furze, and was now baying at the colt and me with mingled terror and indignation. I addressed him in a whisper, with perfidious endearments, advancing a crafty hand towards him the while, made a snatch for the back of his neck, missed it badly, and got him by the ragged fleece of his hind quarters as he tried to flee. If I had flayed him alive he could hardly have uttered a more deafening series of yells, but, like a fool, instead of letting him go, I dragged him towards me, and tried to stifle the noise by holding his muzzle. The tussle lasted engrossingly for a few seconds, and then the climax of the nightmare arrived.

Mrs Knox's voice, close behind me, said, 'Let go my dog this instant, sir! Who are you – '

Her voice faded away, and I knew that she also had seen the colt's head.

I positively felt sorry for her. At her age there was no knowing what effect the shock might have on her. I scrambled to my feet and confronted her.

'Major Yeates!' she said. There was a deathly pause. 'Will you kindly tell me,' said Mrs Knox slowly, 'am I in Bedlam, or are you? And *what is that*?'

She pointed to the colt, and that unfortunate animal, recognising the voice of his mistress, uttered a hoarse and lamentable whinny. Mrs Knox felt around her for support, found only furze prickles, gazed speechlessly at me, and then, to her eternal honour, fell into wild cackles of laughter.

So, I may say, did Flurry and I. I embarked on my explanation and broke down; Flurry followed suit and broke down too. Overwhelming laughter held us all three; disintegrating our very souls. Mrs Knox pulled herself together first.

'I acquit you, Major Yeates, I acquit you, though appearances are against you. It's clear enough to me you've fallen among thieves.' She stopped and glowered at Flurry. Her purple bonnet

38

was over one eye. 'I'll thank you, sir,' she said, 'to dig out that horse before I leave this place. And when you've dug him out you may keep him. I'll be no receiver of stolen goods!'

She broke off and shook her fist at him. 'Upon my conscience, Tony, I'd give a guinea to have thought of it myself!'

LYNN DOYLE
St Patrick's Day in the Morning

In my early and unreflective days in the North of Ireland green was to me an ominous and threatening colour. I looked on the ceremonial wearers of it with suspicion and distaste. It suggested secret combination for unlawful ends, rebellion, non-payment of rent, and a tendency towards over-sleeping in the mornings.

It was, however, only the last of these strongly-asserted failings of that body of the population which flaunted the abominable hue at 'set times' that came prominently before my childish attention.

My aunt's servant-maid, Bridget Keefe, the first of our servant-maids that emerges from the mists of my childhood, was a faithful creature, hardworking, and incurably cheerful even on washing days; with good hands for delph, china, and even glass.

I have heard my aunt declare – not to Bridget, for she didn't believe in giving her servants 'too big a notion of themselves' – that during her nine years of service Bridget broke only four cups, two plates, a vegetable dish, and five tumblers.

But there was a green streak in Bridget, or such my aunt esteemed it. One serious imperfection she suffered from. Bridget was not a beauty – a good maid seldom is – but she was a fabulous sleeper, noiseless, but profound. Unfortunately, her accomplishment reached its most abysmal depth of oblivion about the time when she ought to have been getting up.

My aunt, who was wakerife herself, and possible a little envious of Bridget's gift of slumber, used to fume and occasionally rage about it. But, in spite of some small asperities of manner and speech, my aunt was at heart kind and long-suffering; and besides, good maids were hard to get in the country. She forgave Bridget unto seventy times seven; or, to be rigidly accurate, unto nine times three hundred and thirteen.

It wasn't the three hundred and thirteen mornings in the year that Bridget had to be divorced from bed as the patient sculptor disinters a human figure from its block of marble. No; what broke my aunt's heart, was, that fifty-two Sunday mornings in the year, Bridget, entirely without the assistance of the alarm clock, rose from her somewhat defective mattress like a lark springing on eager wings from dew-impearled grass. My aunt used to follow the green ribbons to the corner of the road, as Bridget went off to first Mass; and set down the miraculous accomplishment to sheer bigotry.

Yet my aunt suffered patiently for nine years. She considered herself broadminded; and, indeed, according to her lights, so she was. In her heart she respected and approved Bridget's religious devotion. It was through a secular offending, though of the same nature, that we parted with Bridget in the end.

On the sixteenth of a certain March, my aunt had set her mind on travelling to Belfast to buy a Spring hat. By that time of year Spring hats were beginning to nest in the imaginations of farmers' wives in our neighbourhood; and there was no telling when such a portent might hatch out and flutter into church at morning service, causing one of the seven deadly sins to sit up and open her eyes.

My aunt had determined to be in the very first flight; and nothing but a Belfast hat would content her. It was a matter of the first train, an early start on a stormy morning, with over four miles to drive. But three-and-sixpence was three-and-sixpence; and one sacrificed at least ninepence worth of the day by waiting for the second train.

I was not present to see all that happened on that fateful morning (for it was no less), but I was a tolerably observant child, and I think I can reconstruct it: how Bridget, anxious, and interested in hats herself, sat up in bed untimely, yawned, stretched herself, then, looking at the pale square of window, decided that the hour was not yet come, threw herself, as it were, on the bosom of that Cassandra, the alarm clock, and sank back into the blankets and slumber.

Then, my aunt's frantic knuckles on Bridget's door, incautiously seconded, for one time only, by her naked toes; Bridget's conscience-stricken moan and leap for her clothing; the lighting of the range fire, with sticks, newspapers and coal fighting for supremacy in the grate, and Bridget growing more like a negress than an Irishwoman with every dab at her tumbling hair; my aunt's exits and entrances, almost simultaneous, during this performance, until, finally, she remained long enough away –

probably through some difference of opinion with whalebone – for Bridget to get at the paraffin oil jar; a match with a head as unstable as Bridget's own; a friendly blending of warm air and paraffin during the delay; then a whap! of an explosion that rattled the very shelves of the oven, and made charcoal of Bridget's St Patrick's Day fringe.

Then, there was the breakfast; the diversely cooked bacon, compounded of the three better-than-half-cooked slices, the slice that tumbled over the edge of the frying-pan and missed complete cremation by seconds, and the slice that fell on the kitchen floor and lay there half-a-dozen inches from the muzzle of a cat far too scared to put out a paw towards it. That would be the slice that my uncle (an irascible man) turned over by fortunate accident and straightway threw out of the window, along with his fork.

There was the tea, floating half-soaked on water that the kettle had been very much surprised to hear was boiling; the plateful of butter hastily quarried with the handle of a tablespoon. Bridget found her thumb-mark, with the adjoining territory of butter, sticking on the wall after my uncle had dashed off with my aunt in the trap, at a canter.

There was the electricity charged journey to B– station, with my aunt, her fingers to her ears, only kept from crying by her desperate resolve to look her best when she was trying on the new hat; the too-distant prospect of the station and a motionless but very ebullient-looking train; the change of canter into gallop; my uncle's climax of language, and my aun't ultimate disregard of her soul in the effort to keep her body in the trap; the slow, inexorable 'Woof! Woof! Woof!' of the engine; the placid balloons of white smoke floating up from behind the goods-shed.

My aunt travelled to Belfast by the second train. It was too late. The train that had skipped from one to another of her tears that morning had borne to Belfast a neighbour of ours – a faithful wife who kept her house spotless, but my aunt didn't like her. And just as my aunt reached J–'s – 'the shop with style' – and unwontedly perceived that the very first hat her eyes lighted on in the window was the hat of the world, it was reverently lifted from its perch and taken inside.

It did not come out again. My aunt couldn't bear to go in. She waited long, then turned away. There were other head coverings in the window, but no hats. Later in the day she met her enemy, who had a large paper bag in her hand. 'Something told me,' my aunt said afterwards; though she went to church next Sunday hoping against hope, and came home at least outwardly resigned.

You will not be surprised to learn that Bridget quitted our service at the expiration of due legal notice. But you will be wrong in another conclusion. She was not given notice because she overslept on the sixteenth of March; but for quite a different reason.

For almost a year she had been in love with the leading kettle-drummer in the Patrick Sarsfield Flute Band. I always thought the green coats and white knee breeches had something to do with it: though Bridget denied this, and said he was a quare nice fellow, anyway. But on this particular St Patrick's Day the Sarsfield Flute Band was to go past our house on its way to the first train in Belfast. Perhaps the leading kettle-drummer knew the reason; for it was a good quarter of a mile out of their route.

I can only guess what passed through my aunt's mind that morning. She was a kindly woman, as I have said, and sympathetic to young love; and she knew of Bridget's affair of the heart, and favoured it, though she didn't like the green uniform. And though she had been sorely tried, I think that if Bridget had slept-in that morning as well, my aunt would have looked on it as expiation of the previous day's fault, and would have awakened her, in time at least to run after the band and her drummer.

But Bridget did not sleep-in, but rose twenty minutes before the alarm clock sounded, and was dressed in time to go off with the band, and had found leisure amazingly to contrive a fresh fringe.

I do not know what St Patrick himself would have thought of the business. I'm inclined to think he would have sided with Bridget, for he had been a slave himself, and may sometime – before he became a saint, that is – have stolen forty winks on the sides of Slemish. But, anyhow, he wasn't there to intervene on Bridget's behalf; and so we exchanged her for another servant who rose earlier, but might, according to my aunt, just as well have stayed in bed.

Bridget married the drummer later, and went to live with him many miles away; so that I don't know how the pair got on together. But I hope the Sarsfield bandsmen made her husband a wedding present of an old kettle-drum, for the mornings.

SEAMUS O'KELLY
The Rector

The Rector came round the gable of the church. He walked down
the sanded path that curved to the road. Half-way down he
paused, meditated, then turning gazed at the building. It was
square and solid, bulky against the background of the hills. The
Rector hitched up his cuffs as he gazed at the structure. Critical
puckers gathered in little lines across the preserved, peach-like
cheeks. He put his small, nicely-shaped head to one side. There
was a proprietorial, concerned air in his attitude. One knew that
he was thinking of the repairs to the church, anxious about the
gutters, the downpipe, the missing slates on the roof, the painting
of the doors and windows. He struck an attitude as he pondered
the problem of the cracks on the pebble-dashed walls. His
umbrella grounded on the sand with decision. He leaned out a
little on it with deliberation, his lips unconsciously shaping the
words of the ultimatum he should deliver to the Select Vestry.
His figure was slight, he looked old-world, almost funereal,
something that had become detached, that was an outpost, half-
forgotten, lonely; a man who had sunk into a parish where there
was nothing to do. He mumbled a little to himself as he came
down to the gate in the high wall that enclosed the church
grounds.

A group of peasants was coming along the yellow, lonely road,
talking and laughing. The bare-footed women stepped with great
active strides, bearing themselves with energy. They carried heavy
baskets from the market town, but were not conscious of their
weight. The carded-wool petticoats, dyed a robust red, brought a
patch of vividness to the landscape. The white 'bauneens' and
soft black hats of the men afforded a contrast. The Rector's eyes
gazed upon the group with a schooled detachment. It was the
look of a man who stood outside of their lives, who did not expect
to be recognised, and who did not feel called upon to seem
conscious of these peasant folk. The eyes of the peasants were

44

unmoved, uninterested, as they were lifted to the dark figure that stood at the rusty iron gate leading into the enclosed church grounds. He gave them no salutation. Their conversation, voluble, noisy, dropped for a moment, half through embarrassment, half through a feeling that something alive stood by the wayside. A vagueness in expression on both sides was the outward signal that two conservative forces had met for a moment and refused to compromise.

One young girl, whose figure and movements would have kindled the eye of an artist, looked up and appeared as if she would smile. The Rector was conscious of her vivid face, framed in a fringe of black hair, of a mischievousness in her beauty, some careless abandon in the swing of her limbs. But something in the level dark brows of the Rector, something that was dour, forbade her smile. It died in a little flush of confusion. The peasants passed and the Rector gave them time to make some headway before he resumed his walk to the Rectory.

He looked up at the range of hills, great in their extent, mighty in their rhythm, beautiful in the play of light and mist upon them. But to the mind of the Rector they expressed something foreign, they were part of a place that was condemned and lost. He began to think of the young girl who, in her innocence, had half-smiled at him. Why did she not smile? Was she afraid? Of what was she afraid? What evil thing had come between her and that impulse of youth? Some consciousness – of what? The Rector sighed. He had, he was afraid, knowledge of what it was. And that knowledge set his thoughts racing over their accustomed course. He ran over the long tradition of his grievances – grievances that had submerged him in a life that had not even a place in this wayside countryside. His mind worked its way down through all the stages of complaint until it arrived at the *Ne Temere* decree. The lips of the Rector no longer formed half-spoken words; they became two straight, tight little thin lines across the teeth. They would remain that way all the afternoon, held in position while he read the letters in the *Irish Times*. He would give himself up to thoughts of politics, of the deeds of wicked men, of the transactions that go on within and without governments, doping his mind with the drug of class opiates until it was time to go to bed.

Meantime he had to pass a man who was breaking stones in a ditch by the roadside. The hard cracks of the hammer were resounding on the still air. The man looked up from his work as the Rector came along; the grey face of the stone-breaker had a

45

melancholy familiarity for him. The Rector had an impulse – it was seldom he had one. He stood in the centre of the road. The *Ne Temere* decree went from his mind.

'Good-day, my man,' he said, feeling that he had made another concession, and that it would be futile as all the others.

'Good-day, sir,' the stone-breaker made answer, hitching himself upon the sack he had put under his haunches, like one very ready for a conversation.

There was a pause. The Rector did not know very well how to continue. He should, he knew, speak with some sense of colloquialism if he was to get on with this stone-breaker, a person for whom he had a certain removed sympathy. The manner of these people's speech was really a part of the grievances of the Rector. Their conversation, he often secretly assured himself, was peppered with Romish propaganda. But the Rector made another concession.

'It's a fine day, thank God,' he said. He spoke like one who was delivering a message in an unfamiliar language. 'Thank God' was local, and might lend itself to an interpretation that could not be approved. But the Rector imported something into the words that was a protection, something that was of the pulpit, that held a solemnity in its pessimism.

'A fine day, indeed, glory be to God!' the stone-breaker made answer. There was a freshness in his expression, a cheerfulness in the prayer, that made of it an optimism.

The Rector was so conscious of the contrast that it gave him pause again. The peach-like colouring on the cheeks brightened, for a suspicion occurred to him. Could the fellow have meant anything? Had he deliberately set up an optimistic Deity in opposition to the pessimistic Deity of the Rector? The Rector hitched up the white cuffs under his dark sleeves, swung his umbrella, and resumed his way, his lips puckered, a little feverish agitation seizing him.

'A strange, down-hearted kind of a man,' the stone-breaker said to himself, as he reached out for a lump of limestone and raised his hammer. A redbreast, perched on an old thorn bush, looking out on the scene with curious eyes, stretched his wing and his leg, as much as to say, 'Ah, well,' sharpened his beak on a twig, and dropped into the ditch to pick up such gifts as the good earth yielded.

The Rector walked along the road pensive, but steadfast, his eyes upon the alien hills, his mind travelling over ridges of problems that never afforded the gleam of solution. He heard a shout of a laugh. Above the local accents that held a cadence of the Gaelic speech he heard the sharp clipped Northern accent of his own gardener and general factotum. He had brought the man with him when he first came to Connacht, half as a mild form of colonisation, half through a suspicion of local honesty. He now saw the man's shaggy head over the Rectory garden wall, and outside it were the peasants.

How was it that the gardener got on with the local people? How was it that they stood on the road to speak with him, shouting their extravagant laughter at his keen, dry Northern humour?

When he first came the gardener had been more grimly hostile to the place than the Rector himself. There had been an ugly row on the road, and blows had been struck. But that was some years ago. The gardener now appeared very much merged in the life of the place; the gathering outside the Rectory garden was friendly, almost a family party. How was it to be accounted for? Once or twice the Rector found himself suspecting that at the bottom of the phenomenon there might be all unconscious among these people a spirit of common country, of a common democracy, a common humanity, that forced itself to the surface in course of time. The Rector stood, his lips working, his nicely-shaped little head quivering with a sudden agitation. For he found himself thinking along unusual lines, and for that very reason dangerous lines – frightfully dangerous lines, he told himself, as an ugly enlightenment broke across his mind, warming it up for a few moments and no more. As he turned in the gate at the Rectory it was a relief to him – for his own thoughts were frightening him – to see the peasants moving away and the head of the gardener disappear behind the wall. He walked up the path to the Rectory, the lawn dotted over with sombre yew trees all clipped into the shape of torpedoes, all trained directly upon the forts of Heaven! The house was large and comfortable, the walls a faded yellow. Like the church, it was thrown up against the background of the hills. It had all the sombre exclusiveness that made appeal to the Rector. The sight of it comforted him at the moment, and his mental agitation died down. He became normal enough to resume his accustomed outlook, and before he had reached the end of the path his mind had become obsessed again by the thought of the *Ne Temere* decree. Something should, he felt convinced, be done, and done at once.

He ground his umbrella on the step in front of the Rectory door and pondered. At last he came to a conclusion, inspiration lighting up his faded eyes. He tossed his head upwards.

'I must write a letter to the papers,' he said. 'Ireland is lost.'

DANIEL CORKERY
Joy

Again Nora Kelly rose from the table, at which she had been eating, looked through the window, turned from it, and spoke to her sister, who was busy at the fire:

'When the train was passing Kilcully I said to him, "Look out the window, father, you might never see Cork city again," and he turned on me and said, "Do I want to see it? How did I come into it? What was I thinking of all these years and I walking the streets of it? Tell me that? Little care if I never see it again" – that's what he said, and no, he wouldn't look out.'

Margaret, to whom she had spoken, then came to the window from the fire and said:

'Look at him now, God help us, he don't know where to rest; that's the tenth time he's after examining that cowshed.' And she called out: 'Father, come in; there's a sup of tea here for you, come in or it will be cold on you; haven't you to-morrow or the day after to look at them, they'll be there tomorrow as well as to-night.'

The old man turned around; as will happen in strange surroundings he did not at once spy out the window where the voice had come from; when, however, his eyes rested on it, on his two daughters, it suddenly struck him, as if he had been thinking unwonted thoughts of her, that there was something wanting in Margaret's voice. It was a strong voice, with the hard, firm consonants, the pure vowels of the Irish language in it. She was now a middle-aged woman, and although she had lived thirty of her years in the city of Cork, where English is not spoken with any sort of firmness at all, her speech was still full of the strength that would carry up far hillsides, herding cattle or calling to a neighbouring homestead. She was already a full-grown girl when her father's house in Carrignadoura in rock-strewn Iveleary was levelled with the ground on a terrible night of wind and fire, bloodshed and marching men. Perhaps it was that one night,

49

rather than the previous years of growth in that dis-peopled land, which had fixed the temper of her mind, hardening it, making it incapable of being wrought upon by the dilly-dally of the city. Curious, then, that now, heard by him for the first time in thirty years in rural surroundings, the voice struck her father as being somewhat rough and hard; its accent did not chime with his thoughts. But it was only a passing fancy. She had always been the love of his heart, and was that now more than ever. He smiled back at the two women brightly; they were so happy-looking in the fresh-painted window-frame of the brand-new house that the Estate Commissioners had built for him – he smiled back at them, waving his stick and quaintly doffing his hat, as he had seen the grand folk in the city do. But he had no intention of going in to them. Half the farmyard he had not yet examined. Many of the beasts were still unfamiliar to him; he knew he was mixing them up, one with another. The boundaries of the farm were laid along a ridge of trees; and as yet he had not got near that ridge. He could scarcely tear himself away from the yard. Better to him than the drinking of wine were the smell and the sight of the beasts as they lurched, almost fiercely, into the milking stalls, or stood around outside, their nostrils spreading with expectancy, their hoofs stamping impatiently on the hard ground. He had been so long away from all that, cooped up in the city, separated from every one of the intimate sounds, smells, sights, that had helped to create him what he was on that night of passion when he lashed out against armed men! A long exile it had been, and in exile would his days have ended only for the grit of this strong-voiced, middle-aged woman, his daughter. All these years she had been watching the twistings and turnings of the many new laws that were being made from time to time dealing with the land and landlordism; she made her own of them, clause by clause, judgment by judgment. And her task had been her own, no one helping. Nora, her sister, had yielded herself up to the city's influence; she was a young thing when it gripped her; both she and her brothers, one elder, one younger, soon lost whatever hope they had brought with them from Carrignadoura that they would ever again be rooted in the soil. Perhaps they did not greatly care.

No one had helped her then, unless it was the old man; and his help had been fitful, now he would be all brightness, quoting old poems of the Gaelic bards, old prophecies of the Gaelic saints, but at another time he would chide her or laugh at her: 'Rooted in the soil again – we will, child, and there'll be Kings in Tara!'

When at last the farm did come to them it was beyond even Margaret's expectations: eighty acres of prime land watered by the Blackwater, so rich, so kind, that the old man asked himself as he surveyed it whether he would now go back to Carrignadoura if choice were given him. As he went about he was contrasting the two countries – the meagre soil of the west, which had the colour, the smell, the texture of turf, and this deep, well-fattened soil which ran over with prodigality – the condition of the eighteen head of cattle was sufficient to show what it was. While he gazed at these sleek lazy-looking animals, his inner eye was full of the skinny, wiry, daring cattle of the hills. He could hardly believe these cattle were his own; such beasts called up to vision a big house, rich acres, a family of long descent. But this they were, his own – and the rich acres as well, and a house that seemed very big to him when he remembered the dark little hovel in Carrignadoura over which blood had been spilled. And all would be his and his children's and his children's children forever! He glowed with a solemn joy. He could not understand why he felt like sitting down in some quiet place and weeping. To banish the thought he would begin reckoning his riches once again; and so sure as he began, the past would once more become alive. He would recall the names, the appearances of the others who were evicted with him on that far-off night of marching men, of blazing roofs and stampeding cattle. None of them, so far as he knew, had been reinstated. They had no daughter like his Margaret. They were scattered to the four winds. It had been like a second Famine to them – child had drifted away from father, husband from wife, brother from sister. What he would give to be able to gather round him now even a few of these lost companions! But they were gone forever. He turned to where the hedge skirted the bohereen. There, to his astonishment, a dark-featured man was staring at him, staring steadily, with meaning and wonder it seemed. He stared in return. It was Tadhg Kearney from Tooreenanean! – a man he had not seen even once since that far-off night of struggle. 'Tadhg! Tadhg' he called – 'Is it you?' But he couldn't wait for an answer. 'Look,' and his stick swept round the bawn fields – 'all mine, and these yonder as well – and the cattle!' How would Tadhg Kearney, proud man, take that? He turned to watch him. But . . . He went forward. What he had taken for a dark-featured man was nothing but an old stump of a tree that stood up from the brosna of the hedge. He went right up

51

to it. 'God leave me the senses,' he said, and he poked at the trunk with the tip of his stick, as one does to a beast at a fair. And he smiled. But almost immediately he grew solemn and anxious again. 'I'm after thanking You, O Christ, on my bended knees,' he muttered, his hat in his hand. 'O Christ, King of Sunday, and you too, Mother of the Son of God, Mary of the Graces.'

More quietly, more contained than before, he wandered from place to place; he did not now look at one thing more than another, yet all the time he was deeply conscious of the peace that was around him, the fatness, the well-being, the golden evening, the peace.

Under far-spreading boughs of great beechen boles he wandered; the ash-grey trunks were stouter than the great pillars he had seen in the big churches in the city. Low gleams of red sunshine shooting wilfully here and there turned the deep grass and the flowers and the brushwood to a rich golden colour – the colour of altar vessels. It was a fairy land to one who had grown up in Iveleary, where few trees are to be seen except the birth, the rowan, the holly – shrunken trees, meagre of foliage. Suddenly he stopped. He had heard merry voices; he listened; the air was full of them – a call, a cry, a ringing cheer, overtaking one another, mingling, separating. He crept slyly nearer. He came upon a well-kept path – it was dappled with sun and shadow. Almost as he discovered it, two Dominicans, very tall, very stately in their long robes of white and black, swept swiftly by, their hands were hidden in their sleeves, their voices were low, their faces earnest. They were gone! They had not seen him, although he had clutched his hat from his head and bowed with reverence. He felt a little dazed. Perhaps he had not seen them at all – he remembered the tree-trunk, how he had taken it for Tadhg Kearney. He caught hold of a slender ash-bole and leaned out into the pathway. Yes, there were the two figures, with the sun and shadow playing upon their backs as they went along the wide avenue. And others were coming. He withdrew into the shade. Looking beyond the path, he saw wide, level fields, crowded with brightly-clad youthful figures: they were hurling. It was from these the merry cries had come. To his right, through a screen of thin foliage, he caught sight of sun-white walls, buttresses, carved stones – many buildings, one of them a church; the windows were tipped with fire. It was all very unexpected, beautiful, radiant. Old poems swept into his mind, poems that were written

52

in the darkest years of the eighteenth century when nothing except hope was left the Gael. Such an Ireland as this he had come upon to-day they had prophesied. 'The laws of Rome will be in practice – religion without blemish' – would be a literal rendering of two of the lines that swept upon him; over and over he recited them, for the Irish words were full of bright music and deftness. But a bell clanged with authority, and the figures went from the fields; he saw the priests crossing the playing field diagonally. And then it seemed to him that a band of music had suddenly ceased!

Excited, he turned to retrace the way he had come. He felt he needed to rest; he had had too many impressions in too short a time. He would sit quietly by the hearth and take out his beads. That would be best. He drew as swiftly as he could towards the farmyard. But again he was perplexed. And he began to fear for himself. There, too, were merry voices, seemingly a host of them – not in the farmyard, the farmyard was deserted. Through it he went. A door opened: he heard a ringing voice giving out fine words and phrases: 'To the Gaelic race the riches of the air above it, the soil within it, the seas around it!' He could hear no more for the shout of approval. 'Rooted in the soil for ever, as the love of Ireland in our hearts!' was the next phrase he caught up. He hastened on. In other years he had heard such phrases, only instead of ringing with the pride of victories gained, they had rung with the hatred of dispossessed people. 'Who shall rule us but ourselves – who is fit for it?' His heart gave a leap; he made to enter the house. It was crowded with men. He then went around to the front. On the roadway, mounted on a car which had been roughly decked with green boughs, was the orator – a man with a shining forehead, and eyes full of the pride of race. Everywhere were green boughs; everywhere, too, green flags with inscriptions in red gold upon them. He saw a crowd of golden instruments. And all the time the high-hearted phrases were ringing in his ears - – the myriad love-names of Ireland were invoked. Each had its own association – the Little Dark Rose, the Sean Bhean Bhocht, the Silk of the Kine, Innisfail, the Plain of Conn, Fodla, Banba – they were as so many stops on an organ. Not one of them but set old songs of the Gael stirring in his memory. He trembled with excitement. Only his anxiety to hear everything, to understand everything, kept him alive, he felt. And his thought renewed to him the priests walking in the avenue, the brightly-clad figures on the green, the sun-tipped windows. And the rich under-foliage, the great boles, the wide branches. He clutched his forehead: his name had been put into the discourse, he heard the words 'His fight at Carrignadoura!' He was being seized and dragged forward – but his daughter Margaret and his daughter Nora were near him, and his son John was helping him – and all the faces about him were those of men who had fought and won. As if by an afterthought, somebody took the hat from his head: there was a deafening outburst of cheering, it was more like a roar – his locks were unexpectedly white. It was as if the people thought of those grey locks as spoil from that distant battle field. The roar redoubled; it would never end. There was confusion, too. His thoughts were going astray. A young man stood before him: he was speaking in Irish: he had never seen a young man look so handsome, so proud. He looked like a king's son. The old man wouldn't dare to reply; his limbs were quivering, he turned away, he drew down his daughter's head. 'What is it?' she said. 'Are there Kings in Tara?' he whispered, in an excited voice, breathy, warm, husky.

When the triumph was over, when the music had died away along the road, and no one remained in the house except the old man and his children, they began to chaff him on the great reception he had had. He struggled with them good-humouredly.

'You haven't it right,' he said, 'you haven't it right at all.'

'Haven't we now? Haven't we now?' his son kept tormenting him.

'No; you haven't; that isn't what I was thinking about at all.'

'Isn't it now; maybe 'twas something grander then?'

'It wasn't.'

'What was it?'

'I asked Margaret here about the Kings – '

'You did – '

'Well, and if she said "Yes" instead of "No" what was it I had in my mind, do you think?'

They stood up and laughed – his head was thrust out so earnestly.

'Well, what had you in your mind?'

'You won't understand.'

'We'll try – '

He gestured with his stick.

'The best of them beasts outside – I'd send him the road to Tara – 'tis long since I had anything to give anybody.'

He took out his beads and they knelt for the night prayers.

It was a rich night in autumn; the earth was fruiting.

JAMES STEPHENS
Desire

1

He was excited, and as he leaned forward in his chair and told this story to his wife he revealed to her a degree or a species of credulity of which she could not have believed him capable.

He was a level-headed man, and habitually conducted his affairs on hard-headed principles. He had conducted his courtship, his matrimonial and domestic affairs in a manner which she should not have termed reckless or romantic. When, therefore, she found him excited, and over such a story, she did not know how just to take the matter.

She compromised by agreeing with him, not because her reason was satisfied or even touched, but simply because he was excited, and a woman can welcome anything which varies the dull round and will bathe in exclamations if she gets the chance.

This was what he told her.

As he was walking to lunch a motor car came down the street at a speed too dangerous for the narrow and congested thoroughfare. A man was walking in front of him, and, just as the car came behind, this man stepped off the path with a view to crossing the road. He did not even look behind as he stepped off. Her husband stretched a ready arm that swept the man back to the pavement one second before the car went blaring and buzzing by.

'If I had not been there,' said her husband, who liked slang, 'you would have got it where the chicken got the axe.'

The two men grinned at each other; her husband smiling with good-fellowship, the other crinkling with amusement and gratitude.

They walked down the street and, on the strength of that adventure, they had lunch together.

They had sat for a long time after lunch, making each other's acquaintance, smoking innumerable cigarettes, and engaged in a conversation which she could never have believed her husband would have shared in for ten minutes; and they had parted with a wish, from her husband, that they should meet again on the following day, and a wordless smile from the man.

He had neither ratified nor negatived the arrangement.

'I hope he'll turn up,' said her husband.

This conversation had excited her man, for it had drawn him into an atmosphere to which he was a stranger, and he had found himself moving there with such pleasure that he wished to get back to it with as little delay as possible.

Briefly, as he explained it to her, the atmosphere was religious, and while it was entirely intellectual it was more heady and exhilarating than the emotional religion to which he had been accustomed, and from which he had silently lapsed.

He tried to describe his companion; but had such ill success in the description that she could not remember afterwards whether he was tall or short; fat or thin; fair or dark.

It was the man's eyes only that he succeeded in emphasising; and these, it appeared, were eyes such as he had never before seen in a human face.

That also, he amended, was a wrong way of putting it, for his eyes were exactly like everybody else's. It was the way he looked through them that was different. Something, very steady, very ardent, very quiet and powerful, was using these eyes for purposes of vision. He had never met anyone who looked at him so . . . comprehendingly; so agreeably.

'You are in love,' said she with a laugh.

After this her husband's explanations became more explanatory but not less confused, until she found that they were both, with curious unconsciousness, in the middle of a fairy-tale.

'He asked me,' said her husband, 'what was the thing I wished for beyond all things.

'That was the most difficult question I have ever been invited to answer,' he went on; 'and for nearly half an hour we sat thinking it out, and discussing magnificences and possibilities.

'I had all the usual thoughts; and, of course, the first of them was wealth. We are more dominated by proverbial phrases than we conceive of, and, such a question being posed, the words "Healthy, wealthy, and wise" will come, unbidden, to answer it. To be alive is to be acquisitive, and so I mentioned wealth, tentatively, as a possibility; and he agreed that it was worth considering. But after a while I knew that I did not want money.'

'One always has need of money,' said his wife.

'In a way, that is true,' he replied, 'but not in this way; for, as I thought it over, I remembered that we have no children; and that our relatively few desires, or fancies, can be readily satisfied by the money we already have. Also we are fairly well off; we have enough in the stocking to last our time even if I ceased from business, which I am not going to do; and, in short, I discovered that money or its purchasing power had not any particular advantages to offer.'

'All the same!' she murmured; and halted with her eyes fixed on purchasings far away in time and space.

'All the same!' he agreed with a smile.

'I could not think of anything worth wishing for,' he continued. 'I mentioned health and wisdom, and we considered these; but, judging myself by the standard of the world in which we move, I concluded that both my health and knowledge were as good as the next man's; and I thought also that if I elected to become wiser than my contemporaries I might be a very lonely person for the rest of my days.'

'Yes,' said she thoughtfully, 'I am glad you did not ask to be made wise, unless you could have asked it for both of us.'

'I asked him in the end what he would advise me to demand, but he replied that he could not advise me at all. 'Behind everything stands desire,' said he, 'and you must find out your desire.'

'I asked him then, if the condition were reversed and if the opportunity had come to him instead of to me, what he should have asked for; not, as I explained to him, in order that I might copy his wish, but from sheer curiosity. He replied that he should not ask for anything. This reply astonished, almost alarmed me at first, but most curiously satisfied me on considering it, and I was about to adopt that attitude – '

'Oh,' said his wife.

'When an idea came to me. "Here I am," I said to myself, "forty-eight years of age: rich enough; sound enough in wind and limb; and as wise as I can afford to be. What is there now belonging to me, absolutely mine, but from which I must part, and which I should like to keep?" And I saw that the thing which was leaving me day by day; second by second; irretrievably and inevitably; was my forty-eighth year. I thought I should like to continue at the age of forty-eight until my time was up.

'I did not ask to live for ever, or any of that nonsense, for I saw that to live for ever is to be condemned to a misery of boredom more dreadful than anything else the mind can conceive of. But, while I do live, I wish to live competently, and so I asked to be allowed to stay at the age of forty-eight years with all the equipment of my present state unimpaired.'

'You should not have asked for such a thing,' said his wife, a little angrily. 'It is not fair to me,' she explained. 'You are older than I am now, but in a few years this will mean that I shall be needlessly older than you. I think it was not a loyal wish.'

'I thought of that objection,' said he, 'and I also thought that I was past the age at which certain things matter; and that both temperamentally and in the matter of years I am proof against sensual or such-like attractions. It seemed to me to be right; so I just registered my wish with him.'

'What did he say?' she queried.

'He did not say anything; he just nodded; and began to talk again of other matters – religion, life, death, mind; a host of things, which, for all the diversity they seem to have when I enumerate them, were yet one single theme.

'I feel a more contented man to-night than I have ever felt,' he continued, 'and I feel in some curious way a different person from the man I was yesterday.'

Here his wife awakened from the conversation and began to laugh.

'You are a foolish man,' said she, 'and I am just as bad. If anyone were to hear us talking this solemn silliness they would have a right to mock at us.'

He laughed heartily with her, and after a light supper they went to bed.

2

During the night his wife had a dream.

She dreamed that a ship set away for the Polar Seas on an expedition in which she was not sufficiently interested to find out its reason. The ship departed with her on board. All that she knew or cared was that she was greatly concerned with baggage, and with counting and going over the various articles that she had brought against arctic weather.

She had thick woollen stockings. She had skin boots all hairy inside, all pliable and wrinkled without. She had a great skin cap shaped like a helmet and fitting down in a cape over her shoulders. She had, and they did not astonish her, a pair of very baggy fur trousers. She had a sleeping sack.

She had an enormous quantity of things; and everybody in the expedition was equipped, if not with the same things, at least similarly.

These traps were a continuous subject of conversation aboard, and, although days and weeks passed, the talk of the ship hovered about and fell continually into the subject of warm clothing.

There came a day when the weather was perceptibly colder; so cold that she was tempted to draw on those wonderful breeches, and to fit her head into that most comfortable hat. But she did not do so; for, and everybody on the ship explained it to her, it was necessary that she should accustom herself to the feeling, the experience, of cold; and, she was further assured that the chill which she was now resenting was nothing to the freezing she should presently have to bear.

It seemed good advice; and she decided that as long as she could bear the cold she would do so, and would not put on any protective covering; thus, when the cold became really intense, she would be in some measure inured to it, and would not suffer so much.

But steadily, and day by day, the weather grew colder.

For now they were in wild and whirling seas wherein great green and white icebergs went sailing by; and all about the ship little hummocks of ice bobbed and surged, and went under and came up; and the grey water slashed and hissed against and on top of these small hillocks.

Her hands were so cold that she had to put them under her armpits to keep any warmth in them; and her feet were in a worse condition. They had begun to pain her; so she decided that on the morrow she would put on her winter equipment, and would not mind what anybody said to the contrary.

'It is cold enough,' said she, 'for my arctic trousers, for my warm soft boots, and my great furry gloves. I will put them on in the morning,' for it was then almost night and she meant to go to bed at once.

She did go to bed; and she lay there in a very misery of cold.

In the morning, she was yet colder; and immediately on rising she looked for the winter clothing which she had laid ready by the side of her bunk the night before; but she could not find them. She was forced to dress in her usual rather thin clothes; and, having done so, she went on deck.

When she got to the side of the vessel she found that the world about her had changed.

The sea had disappeared. Far as the eye could peer was a level plain of ice, not white, but dull grey; and over it there lowered a sky, grey as itself and of almost the same dullness.

Across this waste there blew a bitter, a piercing wind that her eyes winced from, and that caused her ears to tingle and sting.

Not a soul was moving on the ship, and the dead silence which brooded on the ice lay heavy and almost solid on the vessel.

She ran to the other side, and found that the whole ship's company had landed, and were staring at her from a little distance of the ship. And these people were as silent as the frozen air, as the frozen ship. They stared at her; they made no move; they made no sound.

She noticed that they were all dressed in their winter furs; and, while she stood, ice began to creep into her veins.

One of the ship's company strode forward a few paces and held up a bundle in his mittened hand. She was amazed to see that the bundle contained her clothes; her broad furry trousers; her great cosy helmet and gloves.

To get from the ship to the ice was painful but not impossible. A rope ladder was hanging against the side, and she went down this. The rungs felt hard as iron, for they were frozen stiff; and the touch of those glassy surfaces bit into her tender hand like fire. But she got to the ice and went across it towards her companions.

Then, to her dismay, to her terror, all these, suddenly, with one unexpressed accord, turned and began to run away from her; and she, with a heart that shook once and could scarcely beat again, took after them.

Every few paces she fell, for her shoes could not grip on the ice; and each time that she fell those monsters stood and turned and watched her, and the man who had her clothes waved the bundle at her and danced grotesquely, silently.

She continued running, sliding, falling, picking herself up, until her breath went, and she came to a halt, unable to move a limb further and scarcely able to breathe; and this time they did not stay to look at her.

They continued running, but now with great and greater speed, with the very speed of madmen; and she saw them become black specks away on the white distance; and she saw them disappear; and she saw that there was nothing where she stared but the long white miles, and the terrible silence, and the cold.

How cold it was!

And with that there arose a noiseless wind, keen as a razor.

It stung into her face; it swirled about her ankles like a lash; it stabbed under her armpits like a dagger.

'I am cold,' she murmured.

She looked backwards whence she had come, but the ship was no longer in sight, and she could not remember from what direction she had come.

Then she began to run in any direction.

Indeed she ran in every direction to find the ship; for when she had taken a hundred steps in one way she thought frantically, 'This is not the way,' and at once she began to run on the opposite road. But run as she might she could not get warm; it was colder she got. And then, on a steel-grey plane, she slipped, and slipped again and went sliding down a hollow, faster and faster; she came to the brink of a cleft, and swished over this, and down into a hole of ice and there she lay.

'I shall die!' she said. 'I shall fall asleep here and die . . . '

Then she awakened.

She opened her eyes directly on the window and saw the ghost of dawn struggling with the ghoul of darkness. A greyish perceptibility framed the window without, but could not daunt the obscurity within; and she lay for a moment terrified at that grotesque adventure, and thanking God that it had only been a dream.

In another second she felt that she was cold. She pulled the clothes more tightly about her, and she spoke to her husband.

'How miserably cold it is!' she said.

She turned in the bed and snuggled against him for warmth; and she found that an atrocity of cold came from him; that he was icy.

She leaped from the bed with a scream. She switched on the light, and bent over her husband –

He was stone dead. He was stone cold. And she stood by him, shivering and whimpering.

61

JAMES JOYCE
The Sisters

There was no hope for him this time; it was the third stroke. Night after night I had passed the house (it was vacation time) and studied the lighted square of window: and night after night I had found it lighted in the same way, faintly and evenly. If he was dead, I thought, I would see the reflection of candles on the darkened blind, for I knew that two candles must be set at the head of a corpse. He had often said to me: 'I am not long for this world,' and I had thought his words idle. Now I knew they were true. Every night as I gazed up at the window I said softly to myself the word paralysis. It had always sounded strangely in my ears, like the word ghomon in the Euclid and the word simony in the Catechism. But now it sounded to me like the name of some maleficent and sinful being. It filled me with fear, and yet I longed to be nearer to it and to look upon its deadly work.

Old Cotter was sitting at the fire, smoking, when I came downstairs to supper. While my aunt was ladling out my stirabout he said, as if returning to some former remark of his:

'No, I wouldn't say he was exactly . . . but there was something queer . . . there was something uncanny about him. I'll tell you my opinion . . . '

He began to puff at his pipe, no doubt arranging his opinion in his mind. Tiresome old fool! When we knew him first he used to be rather interesting, talking of faints and worms; but I soon grew tired of him and his endless stories about the distillery.

'I have my own theory about it,' he said. 'I think it was one of those . . . peculiar cases . . . But it's hard to say . . . '

He began to puff again at his pipe without giving us his theory. My uncle saw me staring and said to me:

'Well, so your old friend is gone, you'll be sorry to hear.'

'Who?' said I.

'Father Flynn.'

'Is he dead?'

'Mr Cotter here has just told us. He was passing by the house.'

I knew that I was under observation, so I continued eating as if the news had not interested me. My uncle explained to old Cotter.

'The youngster and he were great friends. The old chap taught him a great deal, mind you; and they say he had a great wish for him.'

'God have mercy on his soul,' said my aunt piously.

Old Cotter looked at me for a while. I felt that his little beady black eyes were examining me, but I would not satisfy him by looking up from my plate. He returned to his pipe and finally spat rudely into the grate.

'I wouldn't like children of mine,' he said, 'to have too much to say to a man like that.'

'How do you mean, Mr Cotter?' asked my aunt.

'What I mean is,' said old Cotter, 'it's bad for children. My idea is: let a young lad run about and play with young lads of his own age and not be . . . Am I right, Jack?'

'That's my principle, too,' said my uncle. 'Let him learn to box his corner. That's what I'm always saying to that Rosicrucian there: take exercise. Why, when I was a nipper, every morning of my life I had a cold bath, winter and summer. And that's what stands to me now. Education is all very fine and large . . . Mr Cotter might take a pick of that leg of mutton,' he added to my aunt.

'No, no, not for me,' said old Cotter.

My aunt brought the dish from the safe and put it on the table.

'But why do you think it's not good for children, Mr Cotter?' she asked.

'It's bad for children,' said old Cotter, 'because their minds are so impressionable. When children see things like that, you know, it has an effect . . . '

I crammed my mouth with stirabout for fear I might give utterance to my anger. Tiresome old red-nosed imbecile!

It was late when I fell asleep. Though I was angry with old Cotter for alluding to me as a child, I puzzled my head to extract meaning from his unfinished sentences. In the dark of my room I imagined that I saw again the heavy grey face of the paralytic. I drew the blankets over my head and tried to think of Christmas. But the grey face still followed me. It murmured; and I understood that it desired to confess something. I felt my soul receding into some pleasant and vicious region; and there again I found it waiting for me. It began to confess to me in a murmuring voice and I wondered why it smiled continually and why the lips were so moist with spittle. But then I remembered that it had died of paralysis and I felt that I too was smiling feebly, as if to absolve the simoniac of his sin.

The next morning after breakfast I went down to look at the little house in Great Britain Street. It was an unassuming shop, registered under the vague name of *Drapery*. The drapery consisted mainly of children's bootees and umbrellas; and on ordinary days a notice used to hang in the window, saying: *Umbrellas Re-covered*. No notice was visible now, for the shutters were up. A crape bouquet was tired to the door-knocker with ribbon. Two poor women and a telegram boy were reading the card pinned on the crape. I approached and read:

1st July, 1895
The Rev. James Flynn (formerly of St Catherine's Church, Meath Street), aged sixty-five years.
R.I.P.

The reading of the card persuaded me that he was dead and I was disturbed to find myself at check. Had he not been dead I would have gone into the little dark room behind the shop to find him sitting in his arm-chair by the fire, nearly smothered in his great-coat. Perhaps my aunt would have given me a packet of High Toast for him, and this present would have roused him from his stupefied doze. It was always I who emptied the packet into his black snuffbox, for his hands trembled too much to allow him to do this without spilling half the snuff about the floor. Even as he raised his large trembling hand to his nose little clouds of snuff dribbled through his fingers over the front of his coat. It may have been those constant showers of snuff which gave his ancient priestly garments their green faded look, for the red handker-chief, blackened, as it always was, with the snuff-stains of a week, with which he tried to brush away the fallen grains, was quite inefficacious.

I wished to go in and look at him, but I had not the courage to knock. I walked away slowly along the sunny side of the street, reading all the theatrical advertisements in the shop-windows as I went. I found it strange that neither I nor the day seemed in a mourning mood and I felt even annoyed at discovering in myself a sensation of freedom as if I had been freed from something by his death. I wondered at this for, as my uncle had said the night before, he had taught me a great deal. He had studied in the Irish college in Rome and he had taught me to pronounce Latin properly. He had told me stories about the catacombs and about Napoleon Bonaparte, and he had explained to me the meaning of the different ceremonies of the Mass and of the different vestments worn by the priest. Sometimes he had amused himself by putting difficult questions to me, asking me what one should do in certain circumstances or whether such and such sins were mortal or venial or only imperfections. His questions showed me how complex and mysterious were certain institutions of the Church which I had always regarded as the simplest acts. The duties of the priest towards the Eucharist and towards the secrecy of the confessional seemed so grave to me that I wondered how anybody had ever found in himself the courage to undertake them; and I was not surprised when he told me that the fathers of the Church had written books as thick as the *Post Office Directory* and as closely printed as the law notices in the newspaper, elucidating all these intricate questions. Often when I thought of this I could make no answer or only a very foolish and halting one, upon which he used to smile and nod his head twice or thrice. Sometimes he used to put me through the responses of the Mass, which he had made me learn by heart; and, as I pattered, he used to smile pensively and nod his head, now and then pushing huge pinches of snuff up each nostril alternately. When he smiled he used to uncover his big discoloured teeth and let his tongue lie upon his lower lip – a habit which had made me feel uneasy in the beginning of our acquaintance before I knew him well.

As I walked along in the sun I remembered old Cotter's words and tried to remember what had happened afterwards in the dream. I remembered that I had noticed long velvet curtains and a swinging lamp of antique fashion. I felt that I had been very far away, in some land where the customs were strange – in Persia, I thought . . . But I could not remember the end of the dream.

In the evening my aunt took me with her to visit the house of mourning. It was after sunset; but the windowpanes of the houses that looked to the west reflected the tawny gold of a great bank of clouds. Nannie received us in the hall; and, as it would have been unseemly to have shouted at her, my aunt shook hands with her for all. The old woman pointed upwards interrogatively and, on my aunt's nodding, proceeded to toil up the narrow staircase before us, her bowed head being scarcely above the level of the banister-rail. At the first landing, she stopped and beckoned us forward encouragingly towards the open door of the dead-room. My aunt went in, and the old woman, seeing that I hesitated to enter, began to beckon to me again repeatedly with her hand.

I went in on tiptoe. The room through the lace end of the blind was suffused with dusky golden light amid which the candles looked like pale thin flames. He had been coffined. Nannie gave the lead and we three knelt down at the foot of the bed. I pretended to pray but I could not gather my thoughts because the old woman's mutterings distracted me. I noticed how clumsily her skirt was hooked at the back and how the heels of her cloth boots were trodden down all to one side. The fancy came to me that the old priest was smiling as he lay there in his coffin.

But no. When we rose and went up to the head of the bed, I saw that he was not smiling. There he lay, solemn and copious, vested as for the altar, his large hands loosely retaining a chalice. His face was very truculent, grey and massive, with black cavernous nostrils and circled by a scanty white fur. There was a heavy odour in the room – the flowers.

We crossed ourselves and came away. In the little room downstairs we found Eliza seated in the arm-chair in state. I groped my way towards my usual chair in the corner while Nannie went to the sideboard and brought out a decanter of sherry and some wine-glasses. She set these on the table and invited us to take a little glass of wine. Then, at her sister's bidding, she filled out the sherry into the glasses and passed them to us. She pressed me to take some cream crackers also, but I declined because I thought I would make too much noise eating them. She seemed to be somewhat disappointed at my refusal and went over quietly to the sofa, where she sat down behind her sister. No one spoke: we all gazed at the empty fireplace.

My aunt waited until Eliza sighed and then said:

'Ah, well, he's gone to a better world.'

Eliza sighed again and bowed her head in assent. My aunt fingered the stem of her wine-glass before sipping a little.

'Did he . . . peacefully?' she asked.

'Oh, quite peacefully, ma'am,' said Eliza. 'You couldn't tell when the breath went out of him. He had a beautiful death, God be praised.'

'And everything . . . ?'

'Father O'Rourke was in with him a Tuesday and anointed him and prepared him and all.'

'He knew then?'

'He was quite resigned.'

'He looks quite resigned,' said my aunt.

'That's what the woman we had in to wash him said. She said he just looked as if he was asleep, he looked that peaceful and resigned. No one would think he'd make such a beautiful corpse.'

'Yes, indeed,' said my aunt.

She sipped a little more from her glass and said:

'Well, Miss Flynn, at any rate it must be a great comfort for you to know that you did all you could for him. You were both very kind to him, I must say.'

Eliza smoothed her dress over her knees.

'Ah, poor James!' she said. 'God knows we done all we could, as poor as we were – we couldn't see him want anything while he was in it.'

Nannie had leaned her head against the soft-pillow and seemed about to fall asleep.

'There's poor Nannie,' said Eliza, looking at her, 'she's wore out. All the work we had, she and me, getting in the woman to wash him and then laying him out and then the coffin and then arranging about the Mass in the chapel. Only for Father O'Rourke I don't know what we'd done at all. It was him brought us all them flowers and them two candlesticks out of the chapel, and wrote out the notice for the *Freeman's General* and took charge of all the papers for the cemetery and poor James's insurance.'

'Wasn't that good of him?' said my aunt.

Eliza closed her eyes and shook her head slowly.

'Ah, there's no friends like old friends,' she said, 'when all is said and done, no friends that a body can trust.'

'Indeed, that's true,' said my aunt. 'And I'm sure now that he's gone to his eternal reward he won't forget you and all your kindness to him.'

'Ah, poor James!' said Eliza. 'He was no great trouble to us. You wouldn't hear him in the house any more than now. Still, I know he's gone and all to that . . . '

'It's when it's all over that you'll miss him,' said my aunt.

'I know that,' said Eliza. 'I won't be bringing him in his cup of beef tea any more, nor you, ma'am, send him his snuff. Ah, poor James!'

She stopped, as if she were communing with the past, and then said shrewdly:

'Mind you, I noticed there was something queer coming over him latterly. Whenever I'd bring in his soup to him there, I'd find him with his breviary fallen to the floor, lying back in the chair and his mouth open.'

She laid a finger against her nose and frowned; then she continued:

'But still and all he kept on saying that before the summer was over he'd go out for a drive one fine day just to see the old house again where we were all born down in Irishtown, and take me and Nannie with him. If we could only get one of them new-fangled carriages that makes no noise that Father O'Rourke told him about, them with the rheumatic wheels, for the day cheap – he said, at Johnny Rush's over the way there and drive out the three of us together of a Sunday evening. He had his mind set on that . . . . . . Poor James!'

'The Lord have mercy on his soul!' said my aunt.

Eliza took out her handkerchief and wiped her eyes with it. Then she put it back again in her pocket and gazed into the empty grate for some time without speaking.

'He was too scrupulous always,' she said. 'The duties of the priesthood was too much for him. And then his life was, you might say, crossed.'

'Yes,' said my aunt. 'He was a disappointed man. You could see that.'

A silence took possession of the little room and, under cover of it, I approached the table and tasted my sherry and then returned quietly to my chair in the corner. Eliza seemed to have fallen into a deep reverie. We waited respectfully for her to break the silence: and after a long pause she said slowly:

'It was that chalice he broke . . . That was the beginning of it. Of course, they say it was all right, that it contained nothing, I mean. But still . . . They say it was the boy's fault. But poor James was so nervous, God be merciful to him!'

'And was that it?' said my aunt. 'I heard something . . . '

Eliza nodded.

'That affected his mind,' she said. 'After that he began to mope by himself, talking to no one and wandering about by himself. So one night he was wanted for to go on a call and they couldn't find him anywhere. They looked high up and low down; and still they couldn't see a sight of him anywhere. So then the clerk suggested to try the chapel. So then they got the keys and opened the chapel, and the clerk and Father O'Rourke and another priest that was

there brought in a light for to look for him . . . And what do you
think but there he was, sitting up by himself in the dark in his
confession-box, wide-awake and laughing-like softly to himself?'

She stopped suddenly as if to listen. I too listened; but there
was no sound in the house: and I knew that the old priest was
lying still in his coffin as we had seen him, solemn and truculent in
death, an idle chalice on his breast.

Eliza resumed:

'Wide-awake and laughing-like to himself . . . So then, of
course, when they saw that, that made them think that there was
something wrong with him . . . '

LIAM O'FLAHERTY
The Landing

Two old women were sitting on the rocks that lay in a great
uneven wall along the seashore beyond the village of Rundangan.
They were knitting. Their red petticoats formed the only patch of
colour among the grey crags about them and behind them. In
front of them stretched the sea, blue and calm. It sparkled far out
where the sun was shining on it. The sky was blue and empty and
the winds were silent. The only noise came from the sea, near the
shore, where it was just low tide. The water babbled and flopped
along the seaweed on the low rocks that lay afar out, black strips
of rock with red seaweed growing on them. It was a spring
evening and the air was warm and fresh, as if it had just been
sprinkled with eau de cologne or something. The old women were
talking in low voices sleepily as they knitted woollen stockings.
'Ah yes,' said one of them called Big Bridget Conlon, an old
woman of seventy, a woman of great size and strength, with big
square jaws like a man, high cheekbones, red complexion and
wistful blue eyes that always seemed to be in mourning about
something. She made a wedge of a corner of the little black shawl
that was tied about her neck and cleaned out her right ear with it.
'I don't know,' she said, 'why it is, but I always get a pain in that
ear when there's bad weather coming. There it is now, just as if
there was a little stream running along inside in it. My grandmother, God have mercy on her, suffered the same way.'

'Yes,' said the other woman, with a lazy and insincere sigh,
'there is no going against tokens that are sent that way.' The other
woman, Mary Mullen, was only sixty-five and her reddish hair
had not yet turned very grey. She had shifty grey eyes and she was
very thin about the body. She was greatly feared in the fishing
village of Rundangan for her slandering tongue, and her habit of
listening by night at other people's doors to eavesdrop on their
conversation.

'Heh, heh,' said Big Bridget, looking out mournfully at the sea, 'sure, we only live by the Grace of God, sure enough, with the sea always watching to devour us. And yet only for it we would starve. Sure, many a thing is a queer thing, sure enough.' She stuck the end of a knitting needle against her teeth and leaned her head against it. With brooding eyes she looked out at the sea that way, as if she were trying to explain something to herself.

The two old women lapsed into silence again and knitted away. The tide turned and it began to flow. From where the women sat the land stretched out on either side into the sea. To the east of them, it stretched out in high cliffs, and to the west it ran along almost level with the sea for about a mile, a bare stretch of naked grey rock strewn with boulders. Farther west it rose gradually into high cliffs..Now a light breeze crept along the crags in fitful gusts, here and there, irregularly. The women did not notice it.

Then suddenly a sharp gust of wind came up from the sea and blew the old women's petticoats in the air like balloons. It fluttered about viciously for a few moments and then disappeared again. The old women sniffed anxiously and rolled up their knitting by a common impulse before they spoke a word. They looked at one another with furrowed brows.

'What did I say to you, Mary?' said Big Bridget in an awed whisper, in which however there was a weird melancholy note of intense pleasure. She covered her mouth with the palm of her right hand and then made a motion as if she were throwing her teeth at the other woman. It was a customary gesture with her. 'That pain in my ear is always right,' she continued; 'it's a storm sure enough.' 'God between us and all harm,' said Mary Mullen, 'and that man of mine is out fishing with my son Patrick and Stephen Halloran. Good mother of mercy,' she whimpered uneasily as she got to her feet, 'they are the only people out fishing from the whole village and a storm is coming. Amn't I the unfortunate woman? Drowned, drowned they will be.' Suddenly she worked herself into a wild frenzy of fear and lamentation and she spread her hands out towards the sea. Standing on the summit of the line of boulders with her hands stretched out and wisps of her grey hair flying about her face, while the rising and whistling wind blew her red petticoat backwards so that her lean thighs were sharpy outlined, she began to curse the sea and bemoan her fate.

'Oh, God forgive you, woman of no sense,' cried Big Bridget, struggling to her feet with difficulty on account of the rheumatic pains she had in her right hip; 'what is this you are saying?

71

Abandoned woman, don't tempt the sea with your words. Don't talk of drowning.' There was a sudden ferocity in her words that was strangely akin to the rapid charges of the wind coming up from the sea about them, cold, contemptuous and biting, like bullets flying across a battlefield fired by unknown men against others whom they have never met, the fierce and destructive movement of maddened nature, blind, and rejoicing in madness. And Mary Mullen, with her hands outstretched, paid no heed to Big Bridget, but shrieked at the top of her voice, 'Drowned, drowned they will be.' She also seemed to be possessed with a frenzy in which sorrow and joy had lost their values and had intermingled in some emotion that transcended themselves. The sea began to swell and break its back with rivulets of foam.

People came running down to the beach from the village as the storm grew in intensity. They gathered together on the wall of boulders with the two old women. Soon there was a cluster of red petticoats and heads hooded in little black shawls, while the men stood about talking anxiously and looking out to sea towards the west. The sea was getting rougher with every wave that broke along the rocky beach. It began to growl and toss about and make noises as if monstrous teeth were being ground. It became alive and spoke with a multitude of different yells that inspired the listeners with horror and hypnotised them into feeling mad with the sea. Their faces set in a deep frown and their eyes had a distant fiery look in them. They shouted when they spoke to one another. Each contradicted the other. They swore angrily. They strutted about on the boulders with their hands behind their backs; looking at the sea suspiciously as if they thought it was going to rush up each minute and devour them.

Stephen Halloran's wife squatted down on a boulder beside Mary Mullen, and the two women, whose men were out fishing, became the centre of interest. They arrogated to themselves a vast importance from the fact that their men were in danger of death from a common enemy, the sea. Their faces were lengthened with an expression of sorrow, but there was a fierce pride in their sharp eyes that looked out at the sea with hatred, like the wives of ancient warriors who watched on the ramparts of stone forts while their men fought in front with stone battleaxes against the enemy. Stephen Halloran's wife, a weak-featured, pale-faced woman with weak eyes that were devoid of eyelashes and were red around the rims, kept rolling her little head from side to side, as she searched the sea to the west, looking out from under her eyebrows and from under the little black shawl that covered her head.

'Ah yes,' she was saying, as she rocked her head. 'I told him this morning when he was setting his hooks in order, not to attempt to go out, on account of the day that was in it, because it was this day twenty year ago, if anybody remembers it, that my grandfather died of pneumonia.'

'Drowned, drowned, they will be,' shrieked Mary Mullen. She had gone on her two knees on a boulder and she had put on a man's frieze waistcoat. She looked like a diver in it, the way it was buttoned up around her neck and three sizes too big for her.

The crashing of the waves against the cliffs to the east was drowning the wind. The wind came steadily, like the rushing of a big cataract heard at a great distance, but the noises of the sea were continually changing, rising and falling, with the stupendous modulations of an orchestra played by giants. Each sound boomed or hissed or crashed with a horrid distinctness. It stood apart from the other sounds that followed and preceded it as menacing and overwhelming as the visions that crowd on a disordered mind, each standing apart from the others in crazy independence.

Then the curragh with the three men rowing in it hove into sight from the west. A cliff jutted out into the sea, forming a break-water where its sharp wedge-shaped face ended. Around that cliff the curragh appeared, a tiny black dot on the blue and white sea. For a moment the people saw it and they murmured in an awed loud whisper, 'There they are.' Then the curragh disappeared. It seemed to those on the beach that a monstrous wave surrounded it callously and that it had been engulfed and lost for ever, swallowed into the belly of the ocean. The women shrieked and threw their hands across their breasts and some said, 'Oh Blessed Virgin, succour us.' But the men simply said to one another, 'That was the "Wave of the Reaping Hook" that came down on them.' Still the men had their mouths open and they held their breaths and their bodies leaned forward from their hips watching for the curragh to appear again. It did appear and there was an excited murmur: 'Hah, God with them.'

From the promontory where the curragh had just passed there was a lull in the water for a long way and the people could see the curragh coming along it all the time without losing sight of it. They could see the men rowing in it. They said, 'That's Stephen Halloran in the stern. It's a mistake to have him in the stern. He's

73

too weak on his oars for a rough day.' They began to move cautiously down to the brink of the sea, where the curragh would have to effect a landing. As the moment when the curragh would have to risk the landing and the black rocks, on which the three men might be dashed to pieces by the ferocious sea, came near, the men on the beach grew more excited and some shivered. The women began to wail. A great babble of voices rose from the beach, harsh and confused, like the voices of demented people. All gave advice and none took heed of the advice given.

The place where the curragh would have to effect a landing was in the middle of the little cove. It was a jagged rock with a smooth space at the brink of the left-hand corner, where a slab had been cut out of it by a thunderclap a few years before. In calm weather the sea just reached level with the rock at half tide and it was easy to land a curragh there. But now the waves were coming over it like hills that had been overturned and were being rolled along a level plain speedily. The men on the beach stood at the edge of the rock and the line of boulders, fifty yards away from the edge of the sea. Yet the waves were coming to their feet when the sea swelled up. They shook their heads and looked at one another.

Peter Mullen's brother, a lanky man with a lame leg, made a megaphone of his hands and shouted to the men in the curragh, 'Keep away as long as ye can, ye can't come through this sea,' but he couldn't be heard ten yards away on account of the noise of the sea and of the wind. The curragh approached until it was within two hundred yards of the landing-place. The people on the beach could see the faces of the rowers distinctly. Their faces were distorted and wild. Their bodies were taut with fear and they moved jerkily with their oars, their legs stiff against the sides of the boat, their teeth bared. Two hundred yards away they turned their boat suddenly sideways and began to row away from the landing-place. Silence fell on those on the beach. The men looked eagerly out at the boat. The women rose to their feet and clasped one another. For half a minute there was silence that way while the men in the boat manoeuvred for position.

Then simultaneously a cry arose from the men on the beach and from the men in the boat. With a singing sound of oars grating - through the polished wet wood of the gunwale the curragh swung around to the landing. The singing sound of the oars and the ferocious snapping of the men's breath as they pulled could be heard over the roar of the sea, it came so suddenly. The boat swung in towards the rocks. In a few moments the rowers would be smashed to pieces or in safety.

Then the women standing on the boulders became mad with excitement. They did not shrink in fear from looking at the snaky black canvas-coated boat, with three men in her, that was cutting the blue and white water, dashing in on the rocks. They screamed and there was a wild, mad joy in their screams. Big Bridget's eyes were no longer mournful. They were fiery like a man's. All the women except Mary Mullen and Stephen Halloran's wife looked greedily at the curragh, but at the same time they tore their hair and screamed with pretended fear. Mary Mullen fell on her face on the boulder and, resting her chin on her hands, she kept biting her little finger and saying in a whisper to herself, 'Oh noble son of my womb.' Stephen Halloran's wife rolled herself in her shawl low down between two boulders and went into hysterics.

And the men in the rapidly advancing boat yelled too, a mad joyous yell, as if the rapidity of their movement, the roaring of the sea, the hypnotic power of the green and white water about them and the wind overhead screaming had driven out fear. In the moment of delirium when their boat bore down on death they no longer feared death.

The boat, the crew, the men on the beach, the women on the boulder were all mingled together for a wild moment in a common contempt of danger. For a moment their cries surmounted the sound of the wind and sea. It was the defiance of humanity hurled in the face of merciless nature. And then again there was a strained pause. The noise of voices vanished suddenly and silence came.

On the back of a wave the boat came riding in, the oars stretched out, their points tipping the water. Then the oars dipped. There was a creak, a splash, a rushing sound, a panting of frightened breath, a hurried mumble of excited voices rose from the men on the beach. The men on the beach waited in two lines with clasped hands. The foremost men were up to their waist in water. The boat rushed in between the two lines. They seized the boat. The wave passed over their heads. There was a wild shriek and then confusion. The boat and the foremost men were covered by the wave. Then the wave receded. The boat and the crew and the men holding the boat were left on the rock, clinging to the rock and to one another, like a dragged dog clings to the earth.

They rushed up the rock with the boat. They had landed safely.

ELIZABETH BOWEN
A Day in the Dark

Coming into Moher over the bridge, you may see a terrace of
houses by the river. They are to the left of the bridge, below it.
Their narrow height and faded air of importance make them seem
to mark the approach to some larger town. The six dwellings unite
into one frontage, colour-washed apricot years ago. They face
north. Their lower sash windows, front steps and fanlit front
doors are screened by lime trees, making for privacy. There are
area railings. Between them and the water runs a road with a
parapet, which comes to its end opposite the last house.

On the other side of the bridge picturesquely rises a ruined
castle – more likely to catch the tourist's eye. Woods, from which
the river emerges, go back deeply behind the ruin: on clear days
there is a backdrop of Irish-blue mountains. Otherwise Moher has
little to show. The little place prospers – a market town with a
square, on a main road. The hotel is ample, cheerful, and does
business. Moreover Moher is, and has been for ages, a milling
town. Obsolete stone buildings follow you some way along the
river valley as, having passed through Moher, you pursue your
road. The flour-white modern mills, everywhere, hum.

Round the square, shops and pubs are of many colours – in the
main Moher looks like a chalk drawing. Not so the valley with
its elusive lights.

You *could,* I can see, overlook my terrace of houses – because
of the castle, indifference or haste. I only do not because I am
looking out for them. For in No. 4 lived Miss Banderry.

She was the last of a former milling family – last, that is, but
for the widowed niece, her pensioner. She owned the terrace,
drew rents also from property in another part of the town, and
had acquired, some miles out of Moher, a profitable farm which
she'd put to management. Had control of the family mills been
hers, they would not have been parted with – as it was, she had
had to contend with a hopeless brother: he it was who had ended

by selling out. Her demand for her share of the money left him unable to meet personal debts: he was found hanged from one of the old mill crossbeams. Miss Banderry lived in retirement, the more thought of for being seldom seen – now and then she would summon a Ford hackney and drive to her farm in it, without warning. My uncle, whose land adjoined on hers, had dealings with her, in the main friendly – which was how they first fell into talk. She, a formidable reader, took to sending him serious magazines, reviews, pamphlets and so on, with marked passages on which she would be dying to hear his views. This was her way of harrying him. For my uncle, a winning, versatile and when necessary inventive talker, fundamentally hated to tax his brain. He took to evading meetings with her as far as possible.

So much I knew when I rang her doorbell.

It was July, a sunless warm afternoon, dead still. The terrace was heavy with limes in flower. Above, through the branches, appeared the bridge with idlers who leaned on the balustrade spying down upon me, or so I thought. I felt marked by visiting this place – I was fifteen, and my every sensation was acute in a way I recall, yet cannot recall. All six houses were locked in childless silence. From under the parapet came languidly the mesmeric sound of the weir, and, from a window over my head, the wiry hopping of a bird in a cage. From the shabby other doors of the terrace, No. 4's stood out, handsomely though sombrely painted red. It opened.

I came to return a copy of *Blackwood's*. Also I carried a bunch of ungainly roses from my uncle's garden, and a request that he might borrow the thistle cutter from Miss Banderry's farm for use on his land. One rose moulted petals on to her doorstep, then on to the linoleum in the hall. 'Goodness!' complained the niece, who had let me in. 'Those didn't travel well. Overblown, aren't they!' (I thought that applied to her). 'And I'll bet,' she said, '*he* never sent those!' She was not in her aunt's confidence, being treated more or less like a slave. Timed (they said) when she went on errands into the town – she dare not stay talking, dare not so much as look into the hotel bar while the fun was on. For a woman said to be forty, this sounded mortifying. Widowed Nan, ready to be handsome, wore a cheated ravenous look. It was understood she would come into the money when the aunt died: she must contain herself till then. As for me – how dared she speak of my uncle with her bad breath?

Naturally he *had* never thought of the roses. He had commissioned me to be gallant for him any way I chose, and I would not do too badly with these, I'd thought, as I unstrangled them from the convolvulus in the flowerbed. They would need not only to flatter but to propitiate, for this copy of *Blackwood's* I brought back had buttery thumbmarks on its margins and on its cover a blistered circle where my uncle must have stood down his glass. 'She'll be mad,' he prophesied. 'Better say it was you.' So I sacrificed a hair ribbon to tie the roses. It rejoiced me to stand between him and trouble.

'Auntie's resting,' the niece warned me, and put me to wait. The narrow parlour looked out through thick lace on to the terrace, which was reflected in a looking-glass at the far end. Ugly though I could see honourable furniture, magohany, had been crowded in. In the middle, a circular table wore a chenille cloth. This room felt respected though seldom entered – however, it was peopled in one way: generations of oil-painted portraits hung round the walls, photographs overflowed from bracket and ledge even on to the centre table. I was faced, wherever I turned, by one or another member of the family which could only be the vanished Banderrys. There was a marble clock, but it had stopped.

Footsteps halted heavily over the ceiling, but that was all for I don't know how long. I began to wonder what those Banderrys saw – lodging the magazing and roses on the table, I went to inspect myself in the glass. A tall girl in a sketchy cotton dress. Arms thin, no sign yet of a figure. Hair forward over the shoulders in two plaits, like, say my uncle, a Red Indian maiden's. Barbie was my name.

In memory, the moment before often outlives the awaited moment. I recollect waiting for Miss Banderry – then, nothing till she was with me in the room. I got over our handshake without feeling. On to the massiveness of her bust was pinned a diamond-studded enamelled watch, depending from an enamelled bow: there was a tiny glitter as she grew breath. – 'So he sent *you*, did he?' She sat down, the better to take a look at me. Her apart knees stretched the skirt of her dress. Her choleric colouring and eyeballs made her appear angry, as against which she favoured me with a racy indulgent smile, to counteract the impression she knew she gave.

'I hear wonders of you,' said she, dealing the lie to me like a card.

She sat in reach of the table. 'My bouquet, eh?' She grasped the bundle of roses, thorns and all, and took a long voluptuous sniff at them, as though deceiving herself as to their origin – showing me she knew how to play the game, if I didn't – then shoved back the roses among the photographs and turned her eyes on the magazine, sharply. 'I'm sorry, I – ' I began. In vain. All she gave was a rumbling chuckle – she held up to me the copy of *Blackwood's* open at the page with the most thumbmarks. 'I'd know *those* anywhere!' She scrutinised the print for a line or two. 'Did he make head or tail of it?'

'He told me to tell you, he enjoyed it.' (I saw my uncle dallying, stuffing himself with the buttered toast.) 'With his best thanks.'

'You're a little echo,' she said, not discontentedly.

I stared her out.

'Never mind,' she said. 'He's a handsome fellow.'

I shifted my feet. She gave me a look.

She observed: 'It's a pity to read at table.'

'He hasn't much other time, Miss Banderry.'

'Still, it's a poor compliment to you!'

She stung me into remarking: 'He doesn't often.'

'Oh, I'm sure you're a great companion for him!'

It was as though she saw me casting myself down by my uncle's chair when he'd left the room, or watching the lassitude of his hand hanging caressing a dog's ear. With him I felt the tender bond of sex. Seven, eight weeks with him under his roof, among the copper beeches from spring to summer turning from pink to purple, and I was in love with him. Such things happen, I suppose. He was my mother's brother, but I had not known him when I was a child. Of his manhood I had had no warning. Naturally growing into love I was, like the grass growing into hay on his uncut lawns. There was not a danger till she spoke.

'He's glad of company now and then,' I said as stupidly as I could.

She plucked a petal from her black serge skirt.

'Well,' she said, 'thank him for the thanks. And you for the nice little pleasure of this visit. – Then, there's nothing else?'

'My uncle wants – ' I began.

'You don't surprise me,' said Miss Banderry. 'Well, come on out with it. What this time?'

'If he could once more borrow the thistle cutter . . . ?'

' "Once more"! And what will be looking to do next year. Get his own mended? I suppose he'd hardly go to that length.'

His own, I knew, had been sold for scrap. He was sometimes

looking for ready money. I said nothing.

'Looking for me to keep him out of jail?' (Law forbids one to suffer the growth of thistles.) 'Time after time, it's the same story. It so happens, I haven't mine cut yet!'

'He'd be glad to lend you his jennet back, he says, to draw the cutter for you.'

'*That* brute! There'd be nothing for me to cut if it wasn't for what blows in off his dirty land.' With the flat of her fingers she pressed one eyeball, then the other, back into her head. She confessed, all at once almost plaintively: 'I don't care to have machinery leave my farm.'

'Very well,' I said haughtily, 'I'll tell him.'

She leaned back, rubbed her palms on her thighs. 'No, wait – this you may tell my lord. Tell him I'm not sure but I'll think it over. There might be a favourable answer, there might not. If my lord would like to know which, let him come himself. – That's a sweet little dress of yours,' she went on examining me inside it, 'but it's skimpy. He should do better than hide behind *those* skirts!'

'I don't know what you mean, Miss Banderry.'

'He'd know.'

'Today, my uncle *was* busy.'

'I'm sure he was. Busy day after day. In my life, I've known only one other man anything like so busy as your uncle. And shall I tell you who that was? My poor brother.'

After all these years, that terrace focuses dread. I mislike any terrace facing a river. I suppose I would rather look upon it itself (as I must, whenever I cross that bridge) than be reminded of it by harmless others. True, only one house in it was Miss Banderry's, but the rest belong to her by complicity. An indelible stain is on that monotony – the extinct pink frontage, the road leading to nothing but those six doors which the lime trees, flower as they may, exist for nothing but to shelter. The monotony of the weir and the hopping bird. Within that terrace I was in one room only, and only once.

My conversation with Miss Banderry did not end where I leave off recording it. But at that point memory is torn across, as might be an intolerable page. The other half is missing. For that reason my portrait of her would be incomplete if it *were* a portrait. She could be novelist's material, I daresay – indeed novels, particularly the French and Irish (for Ireland in some ways resembles

80

France), are full of prototypes of her: oversized women insulated in little provinicial towns. Literature, once one knows it, drains away some of the shockingness out of life. But when I met her I was unread, my susceptibilities were virgin. I refuse to fill in her outline retrospectively: I show you only what I saw at the time. Not what she was, but what she did to me.

Her amorous hostility to my uncle – or was it hostility making use of a farce? – unsheathed itself when she likened him to the brother she drove to death.

When I speak of dread I mean dread, not guilt. That afternoon, I went to Miss Banderry's for my uncle's sake, in his place. It could be said, my gathering of foreboding had to do with my relation with him – yet in that there was no guilt anywhere, I could swear! I swear we did each other no harm. I think he was held that summer, as I was, by the sense that this was a summer like no other and which could never again be. Soon I must grow up, he must grow old. Meanwhile we played house together on the margin of a passion which was impossible. My longing was for him, not for an embrace – as for him, he was glad of companionship, as I'd truly told her. He was a man tired by a lonely house till I joined him – a schoolgirl between schools. All thought well of his hospitality to me. Convention was our safeguard: could one have stronger?

I left No. 4 with ceremony. I was offered raspberry cordial. Nan bore in the tray with the thimble glasses – educated by going visiting with my uncle. I knew refusal would mark a breach. When the glasses were emptied, Nan conducted me out of the presence, to the hall door – she and I stopped aimlessly on the steps. Across the river throve the vast new mills, unabashed, and cars swished across the tree-ridden bridge. The niece showed a reluctance to go in again – I think the bird above must have been hers. She glanced behind her, then conspiratorially at me. 'So now you'll be going to the hotel?'

'No. Why?'

' "Why?" ' she jibed. 'Isn't he waiting for you? Anyway, that's where he is: in there. The car's outside.'

I said: 'But I'm taking the bus home.'

'Now, why ever?'

'I said I would take the bus. I came in that way.'

'You're mad. What, with his car in the square?'

All I could say was: 'When?'

'I slipped out just now,' said the niece, 'since you want to know. To a shop, only. While you were chatting with Auntie.' She laughed, perhaps at her life, and impatiently gave me a push away. 'Get on – wherever you're going to! Anybody would think you'd had bad news!'

Not till I was almost on the bridge did I hear No. 4's door shut.

I leaned on the balustrade, at the castle side. The river, coming towards me out of the distance of woods, washed the bastions and carried a paper boat – this, travelling at uncertain speed on the current, listed as it vanished under the bridge. I had not the heart to wonder how it would fare. Weeks ago, when first I came to my uncle's, here we had lingered, elbow to elbow, looking up-river through the green-hazed spring hush at the far off swan's nest, now deserted. Next I raised my eyes to the splendid battlements, kissed by the sky where they were broken.

From the bridge to the town rises a slow hill – shops and places of business come down to meet you, converting the road into a street. There are lamp posts, signboards, yard gates pasted with layers of bills, and you tread pavement. That day the approach to Moher, even the crimson valerian on stone walls, was filmed by imponderable white dust as though the flourbags had been shaken. To me, this was the pallor of suspense. An all but empty theatre was the square, which, when I entered it at a corner, paused between afternoon and evening. In the middle were parked cars, looking forgotten – my uncle's was nearest the hotel.

The hotel, glossy with green creeper, accounted for one end of the square. A cream porch, figuring the name in gold, framed the doorway – though I kept my back to that I expected at any moment to hear a shout as I searched for the independence of my bus. But where *that* should have waited, I found nothing. Nothing, at this bus end of the square, but a drip of grease on dust and a torn ticket. 'She's gone out, if that's what you're looking for,' said a bystander. So there it went, carrying passengers I was not among to the scenes of safety, and away from me every hope of solitude. Out of reach was the savingness of a house empty. Out of reach, the windows down to the ground open upon the purple beeches and lazy hay, the dear weather of those rooms in and out of which flew butterflies, my cushions on the floor, my blue striped tea mug. Out of reach, the whole of the lenient meaning of my uncle's house, which most filled it when he was not there . . . I did not want to be bothered with him, I think.

82

'She went out on time today, more's the pity.'

Down hung my hair in two weighted ropes as I turned away.

Moher square is oblong. Down its length, on the two sides, people started to come to the shop doors in order to look at me in amazement. They knew who I was and where he was: what should *I* be wanting to catch the bus for? They speculated. As though a sandal chafed me I bent down, spent some time loosening the strap. Then, as though I had never had any other thought, I started in the direction of the hotel.

At the same time, my uncle appeared in the porch. He tossed a cigarette away, put the hand in a pocket and stood there under the gold lettering. He was not a lord, only a landowner. Facing Moher, he was all carriage and colouring: he wore his life like he wore his coat – though, now he was finished with the hotel, a light hint of melancholy settled down on him. He was not looking for me until he saw me.

We met at his car. He asked: 'How was she, the old terror?'

'I don't know.'

'She didn't eat you?'

'No,' I said, shaking my head.

'Or send me another magazine?'

'No. Not this time.'

'Thank God.'

He opened the car door and touched my elbow, reminding me to get in.

SEAN O'FAOLAIN
The Kitchen

It was there again last night; not, I need hardly say, deliberately.
If I had my own way I would never even think of that house or
that city, let alone revisit them. It was the usual pattern. I was in
Cork on some family business, and my business required that
I should walk past the house and, as usual, although it was the
deep middle of the night the kitchen window upstairs was dimly
lit, as if by a lamp turned low, the way my mother used always to
fix it to welcome my father home from night duty. She usually left
a covered saucepan of milk beside the lamp. He would put it on
the stove to heat while he shook the rain from his cape on the red
tiles of the kitchen, hung his uniform on the back of the door and
put on a pair of slippers. He welcomed the hot milk. It rains a lot
in Cork and the night rain can be very cold. Then, as happens in
dreams, where you can walk through walls like a pure spirit and
time gets telescoped, it was suddenly broad daylight, I was
standing in the empty kitchen and that young man was once again
saying to me with a kindly chuckle, 'So this is what all that was
about?' It was five past three in the morning when I sat up and
groped wildly for the bedside light to dispel the misery of those
eight dismissive words that I am apparently never going to be
allowed to forget, even in my sleep.

It is a graceless lump of a house, three storeys high,
rhomboidal, cement-faced, built at the meeting point of a quiet
side street curving out of an open square and a narrow, noisy,
muddy, sunless street leading to one of the busiest parts of the
city. Every day for over twenty years I used to look down into this
narrow street from the kitchen window – down because of the
shop beneath us on the ground floor, occupied in my childhood
by a firm of electrical contractors named Cyril and Eaton. Theirs
was a quiet profession. Later on, when the shop was occupied by
a bootmaker, we could hear his machines slapping below us all
day.

My guess is that the house was built around 1870; anyway, it had the solid, ugly, utilitarian look of the period. Not that my father and mother ever thought it ugly. They would not have known what the word meant. To them, born peasants, straight from the fields, all the word 'beautiful' meant was useful or prolific; all 'ugly' meant was useless or barren – a field that grew bad crops, a roof that leaked, a cow that gave poor milk. So, when they told us children, as they often did, that we were now living in a beautiful house all they meant was that it suited our purposes perfectly. They may also have meant something else: because they had been told that the house had originally been put up by a builder for his own use they considered it prime property, as if they had come into possession of land owned by a gentleman farmer for generations. Few things are more dear to the heart of a peasant than a clean pedigree. It keeps history at bay. Not, of course, that they owned the house, although they sometimes talked dreamily about how they would buy it someday. What a dream! Landless people, in other words people of no substance, they had already gone to the limit of daring by renting it for twenty-six pounds a year, a respectable sum in those days for a man like my father – an ordinary policeman, rank of constable, earning about thirty bob a week.

Their purpose in renting so big a place was to eke out his modest income by taking in the steady succession of lodgers who were ultimately to fill the whole house with the sole exception of the red-tiled kitchen where the six of us lived, cooked, idled or worked. I do not count as rooms the warren of attics high up under the roof where we all, including the slavey (half a crown a week and her keep), slept with nothing between us and the moon but the bare slates. Still, we were not really poor. Knowing no better life, we were content with what we had.

During some forty years this was my parents' home; for even after my brothers and I grew up and scattered to the corners of the compass, and my mother grew too old to go on keeping lodgers, and my father retired, they still held on to it. So well they might! I was looking at my father's discharge papers this morning. I find that when he retired at the age of fifty his pension was £48 10s. 8d. a year. Fortunately he did get a part-time job as a caretaker of a garage at night which brought him in another £25 5s. 5d. a year. Any roof at ten bob a week was nicely within his means. It must also have been a heartbreak to his landlord, who could not legally increase the rent.

One day, however, about a year before I left home – I was the last of us to go – my father got a letter which threatened to end this agreeable state of affairs. When he and my mother had painstakingly digested its legal formalities they found to their horror that the bootmaker downstairs had, as the saying goes, quietly bought the house 'over their heads', and was therefore their new landlord. Now forty-odd years in a city, even in so small a city as Cork, can go a long way towards turning a peasant into a citizen. My father, as a lifelong member of the Royal Irish Constabulary, then admiringly called the Force, had over the years imbibed from his training and from the example of his officers, who were mostly Protestants and Gentlemen, not only a strong sense of military, I might even say of imperial, discipline but a considerable degree of urban refinement. My mother had likewise learned her own proper kind of urban ways, house-pride, such skills as cooking and dressmaking and a great liking for pretty clothes. At times she even affected a citified accent. When they read this letter and stared at one another in fright, all this finery fell from their backs as suddenly as Cinderella's at the stroke of midnight.

They might at that moment have been two peasants from Limerick or Kerry peering timidly through the rain from the door of a thatched hovel at a landlord, or his agent, or some villainous land-grabber driving up their brambled boreen to throw them out on the side of the road to die of cold and starvation. The kitchen suddenly became noisy with words, phrases and names that, I well knew, they could not have heard since their childhood – evictions, bum bailiffs, forcible entry, rights-of-way, actions for trespass, easements, appeals, breaches of covenant, the Land Leaguers, the Whiteboys, Parnell and Captain Boycott, as if the bootmaker downstairs slept with a shotgun by his bed every night and a brace of bloodhounds outside his shop door every day.

Nothing I said to comfort them could persuade them that their bootmaker could not possibly want to evict them; or that, far from being a land-grabber, or even a house-grabber, he was just an ordinary, normal, decent hardworking, city-bred business-man, with a large family of his own toiling beside him at his machines, who, if he wanted anything at all, could not con-ceivably want more than, say, one extra room where he could put another sewing machine or store his leather. And, in fact, as he patiently explained to my father, that was all he did want; or perhaps a little more – two rooms, and access for his girls to our

86

private W.C. on the turn of the stairs. He must have been much surprised to find himself thrown headlong into the heart of a raging rural land war.

I left home that year, so I cannot tell if there was or was not litigation at this first stage of the battle. All I know for certain is that after about a year and a half of argufying, both parties settled for one room and access to the W.C. The rest I was to gather and surmise from their letters to me. These conveyed that some sort of growing peace descended on everybody for about three years, towards the end of which my father died, my mother became the sole occupant and the bootmaker, seeing that he now had only one tenant over his head, and that with expanding business he was even more cramped for space than before, renewed his request for a second room.

At once, the war broke out again, intensified now by the fact that, as my mother saw it, a bloody villain of a land-grabber, and a black Protestant to boot, was trying to throw a lonely, helpless, ailing, defenceless, solitary poor widow woman out on the side of the road to die. The bootmaker nevertheless persisted. It took him about two more years of bitter struggle to get his second room. When he got it he was in possession of the whole of the second floor of his house with the exception of the red-tiled kitchen.

Peace returned, grumbling and growling. Patiently he let another year pass. Then, in the gentlest possible words, he begged that my mother might be so kind, and so understanding, as to allow one of his girls, and only one to enter the kitchen once a day, and only once, for the sole purpose of filling a kettle of water from the tap of her kitchen sink. There was, to be sure, he agreed, another tap downstairs in his backyard – a dank five-foot-square patch of cement – but it stood outside the male workers' outdoor W.C., and she would not, he hoped and trusted, wish any girl to be going out there to get water for her poor little cup of tea? I am sure it was the thought of the girl's poor little cup of tea that softened my mother's heart. She royally granted the humane permission, and at once began to regret it.

She realised that she had given the black villain a toehold into her kitchen and foresaw that the next thing he would want would be to take it over completely. She was right. I can only infer that as the bootmaking business went on expanding, so did the bootmaker's sense of the value of time. At any rate he was soon pointing out to my mother that it was a dreadful expense to him, and a hardship to his staff, to have to close his shop for an hour and a half every day while his workers, including his family, trudged home, in all weathers, some of them quite a long distance, for their midday meal. If he had the kitchen they could eat their lunch, dryshod and in comfort, inside half an hour. He entered a formal request for the kitchen.

Looking back at it now, after the passage of well over a quarter of a century, I can see clearly enough that he thought he was making a wholly reasonable request. After all, in addition to her kitchen my mother still possessed the third floor of the house, containing three fine rooms and a spacious bathroom. One of those rooms could become her kitchen, another remain her bedroom and the third and largest, which she never used, would make a splendid living room, overlooking the square's pleasant enclosure of grass and shrubs, and commanding an open view up to the main thoroughfare of the city – all in all as desirable an apartment, by any standards, as thousands of home-hungry Corkonians would have given their ears to possess.

Unfortunately, if I did decide to think his request reasonable, what I would have to forget, and what he completely failed to reckon with, was that there is not a peasant widow woman from the mountains of west Cork to the wilds of Calabria who does not feel her kitchen as the pulse and centre of her being as a wife and a mother. That red-tiled kitchen had been my mother's nest and nursery, her fireside where she prayed every morning, her chimney corner where she rested every night, the sanctum sanctorum of all her belongings, a place where every stain and smell, spiderweb and mousehole, crooked nail and cracked cup made it the ark of the covenant that she had kept through forty years of sweat and struggle for her lost husband and her scattered children.

Besides, if she lost her kitchen what would she do when the Bottle Woman came, to buy empty bottles at a halfpenny apiece? This was where she always brought her to sit and share a pot of tea and argue over the bottles and talk about the secret doings of Cork. Where could she talk with the Dead Man, collecting her funeral insurance at sixpence a week, if she did not have her warm, red-eyed range where he could take off his damp boots and warm his feet in the oven while she picked him dry of all the gossip of the narrow street beneath her window? She had never in her life locked the front door downstairs except at night. Like the door of any country cottage it was always on the latch for any one of her three or four cronies to shove open and call out to her, 'Are ye there, can I come up?' – at which she would hear their footsteps banging on the brass edgings of the stairs while she hastily began to poke the fire in the range, and fill the kettle for the tea, or stir the pot of soup on the range in preparation for a cosy chat. All her life her neighbours had dropped like that into her kitchen. They would be insulted if she did not invite them into her kitchen. She would not have a crony in the world without her kitchen. Knowing nothing of all this, the bootmaker could argue himself hoarse with her, plead and wheedle with her to accept the shiniest, best-equipped, most modern American-style kitchenette, run by electricity, all white and gleaming chromium. Even if it was three storeys up from the hall door it seemed to him a marvellous exchange for this battered old cave downstairs where she crouched over a range called the Prince Albert, where the tiles were becoming loose, where he could see nothing to look at but a chipped sink, one chair, a table, one cupboard, a couple of old wooden shelves and a sofa with the horsehair coming out of it like a moustache. He might just as well have said to a queen, 'Give me your throne and I'll leave you the palace.' While as for proposing as an alternative that she could keep her old kip of a kitchen if she would only let him make a proper kitchen upstairs for himself, his family and his workers . . .

'Aha, nah!' she would cry at me whenever I visited her; and the older and angrier she became the more did her speech revert to the flat accent of her flat west Limerick, with its long vanishing versts of greasy limestone roads, its fields of rusty reeds, its windrattling alders and its low rain clouds endlessly trailing their Atlantic hair across the sodden plain. 'Is it to take me in the rear he wants to now? To lock me up in the loft? To grind me like corn meal between the upstairs and the downstairs? A room? And then another room? And after that another? And then what? When he'd have me surrounded with noise, and shmoke, and schmells, and darkness and a tick-tack-turrorum all day long? Aha. My mother, and my grandmother before her, didn't fight the landlords, and the agents, and the helmeted peelers with their grey guns and their black battering rams for me to pull down the flag now! It's a true word, God knows it, them Protestants wouldn't give you as much as a dry twig in a rotten wood to light your pipe with it. Well and well do I remember the time ould foxwhiskers, Mister Woodley the parson, died of the grippe away back in Crawmore, and my uncle Phil stole out the night after his funeral to cut a log in his wood! While he was sawing it didn't the moon come out from behind a cloud, and who do you think was sitting on the end of the log looking at him out of his foxy eyes? Out of my kitchen I will not stir until ye carry me out on a board to lie in the clay beside my poor Dinny. And not one single minit before.'

Which was exactly what happened, six years later.

All in all, from start to finish, my mother's land war must have lasted nearly fourteen years. But what is fourteen years to an old woman whose line and stock clung by their fingernails to their last sour bits of earth for four centuries? I am quite sure the poor bootmaker never understood to the day of his death the nerve of time he had so unwittingly touched.

After the funeral it was my last task to empty the house, to shovel away – there is no other word for it – her life's last larés and penates to a junk dealer for thirty shillings. When it was all done I was standing alone in the empty kitchen, where I used to do my homework every evening as a boy, watching her cooking or baking, making or mending, or my father cobbling a pair of shoes for one of us, or sitting at his ease, smoking his pipe, in his favourite straw-bottomed chair, in his grey constabulary shirt, reading the racing news in the pink *Cork Evening Echo*.

As I stood there, I suddenly became aware that a young man was standing in the doorway. He was the bootmaker's son. Oddly enough, I had never spoken to his father, although years ago I had seen him passing busily in and out of his shop, always looking worn and worried, but I had once met this son of his in the mountains of west Cork – fishing? shooting? – and I had found him a most friendly and attractive young fellow. He came forward now, shook hands with me in a warm, manly way and told me how sorry he was for me in my bereavement.

'Your mother was a grand old warrior,' he said, in genuine admiration. 'My father always had the greatest respect for her.'

We chatted about this and that for a while. Then, for a moment, we both fell silent while he looked curiously around the bare walls. He chuckled tolerantly, shook his head several times and said, 'So this is what all that was about?'

At those eight words so kindly meant, so good-humoured, so tolerant, so uncomprehending, a shock of weakness flowed up through me like defeat until my head began to reel and my eyes were swimming.

It was quite true that there was nothing for either of us to see but a red-tiled floor, a smoke-browned ceiling and four tawny distempered walls bearing some brighter patches where a few pictures had hung and the cupboard and the sofa used to stand. The wall to our right had deposited at its base a scruff of distemper like dandruff. The wall to our left gaped at us with parched mouths. He smiled up at the flyspotted bulb in the ceiling. He touched a loose tile with his toe and sighed deeply. All that! About this? And yet, only a few hours before, when I had looked down at her for the last time, withdrawn like a snail into her shrivelled house, I had suddenly found myself straining, bending, listening as if, I afterwards thought, I had been staring into the perspective of a tunnel of time, much as I stared now at him, at one with him in his bewilderment.

I thought I had completely understood what it was all about that morning years ago when they read that letter and so pathetically, so embarrassingly, even so comically revealed their peasants' terror at the power of time. I had thought the old bootmaker's mistake had been his failure to understand the long fuse he had so unwittingly lighted. But now – staring at this good-humoured young man who, if I had said all this to him, would at once have understood and have at once retorted, 'But even so!' – I realised that they, and that, and this, and he and I were all caught in something beyond reason and time. In a daze I shook hands with him again, thanked him again for his sympathy and handed him the keys of victory. I was still dazed as I sat in the afternoon train for Dublin, facing the mile-long tunnel that burrows underneath the city out to the light and air of the upper world. As it slowly began to slide into the tunnel I swore that I would never return.

Since that I must have gone back there forty times, sometimes kidnapped by her, sometimes by my father, sometimes by an anonymous rout of shadowy creatures out of a masked ball and sometimes it is not at all the city I once knew but a fantastically beautiful place of great squares and pinnacled, porphyry buildings with snowy ships drawing up beside marble quays. But, always, whatever the order of my guides, captors or companions, I find myself at the end alone in a narrow street, dark except for its single window and then, suddenly, it is broad daylight and I am in our old kitchen hearing that young man say in his easy way, 'So this is what all that was about?' and I start awake in my own dark, babbling, clawing for the switch. As I sit up in bed I can never remember what it was that I had been babbling, but I do understand all over again what it was all about. It was all about the scratching mole. In her time, when she heard it she refused to listen, just as I do when, in my turn, I hear her velvet burrowing, softer than sand crumbling or snow tapping, and I know well whose whispering I had heard and what she had been saying to me.

She was a grand old warrior. She fought her fight to a finish. She was entirely right in everything she did. I am all for her. Still, when I switch on the bulb over my head I do it only to banish her, to evict her, to push her out of *my* kitchen, and I often lie back to sleep under its bright light lest I should again hear her whispering to me in the dark.

FRANK O'CONNOR
The Babes in the Wood

Whenever Mrs Early made Terry put on his best trousers and gansey he knew his aunt must be coming. She didn't come half often enough to suit Terry, but when she did it was great gas. Terry's mother was dead and he lived with Mrs Early and her son, Billy. Mrs Early was a rough, deaf, scolding old woman, doubled up with rheumatics, who'd give you a clout as quick as she'd look at you, but Billy was good gas too.

This particular Sunday morning Billy was scraping his chin frantically and cursing the bloody old razor while the bell was ringing in the valley for Mass, when Terry's aunt arrived. She came into the dark little cottage eagerly, her big rosy face toasted with sunshine and her hand out in greeting.

'Hello, Billy,' she cried in a loud, laughing voice, 'late for Mass again?'

'Let me alone, Miss Conners,' stuttered Billy, turning his lathered face to her from the mirror. 'I think my mother shaves on the sly.'

'And how's Mrs Early?' cried Terry's aunt, kissing the old woman and then fumbling at the strap of her knapsack in her excitable way. Everything about his aunt was excitable and high-powered; the words tumbled out of her so fast that sometime she became incoherent.

'Look, I brought you a couple of things – no, they're fags for Billy' – ('God bless you, Miss Conners,' from Billy) – 'this is for you, and here are a few things for the dinner.'

'And what did you bring me, Auntie?' Terry asked.

'Oh, Terry,' she cried in consternation, 'I forgot about you.'

'You didn't.'

'I did, Terry,' she said tragically. 'I swear I did. Or did I? The bird told me something. What was he said?'

'What sort of bird was it?' asked Terry. 'A thrush?'

'A big grey fellow?'

'That's the old thrush all right. He sings in our back yard.'

'And what was that he told me to bring you?'

'A boat!' shouted Terry.

It was a boat.

After dinner the pair of them went up to the wood for a walk. His aunt had a long, swinging stride that made her hard to keep up with, but she was great gas and Terry wished she'd come to see him oftener. When she did he tried his hardest to be grown-up. All the morning he had been reminding himself: 'Terry, remember you're not a baby any longer. You're nine now, you know.' He wasn't nine, of course; he was still only five and fat, but nine, the age of his girlfriend Florrie, was the one he liked pretending to be. When you were nine you understood everything. There were still things Terry did not understand.

When they reached the top of the hill his aunt threw herself on her back with her knees in the air and her hands under her head. She liked to toast herself like that. She liked walking; her legs were always bare; she usually wore a tweed skirt and pullover. Today she wore black glasses, and when Terry looked through them he saw everything dark; the wooded hills at the other side of the valley and the buses and cars crawling between the rocks at their feet, and, still farther down, the railway track and the river. She promised him a pair for himself next time she came, a small pair to fit him, and he could scarcely bear the thought of having to wait so long for them.

'When will you come again, Auntie?' he asked. 'Next Sunday?'

'I might,' she said and rolled on her belly, propped her head on her hands, and sucked a straw as she laughed at him. 'Why? Do you like it when I come?'

'I love it.'

'Would you like to come and live with me altogether, Terry?'

'Oh, Jay, I would.'

'Are you sure now?' she said, half ragging him. 'You're sure you wouldn't be lonely after Mrs Early or Billy or Florrie?'

'I wouldn't, Auntie, honest,' he said tensely. 'When will you bring me?'

'I don't know yet,' she said. 'It might be sooner than you think.'

'Where would you bring me? Up to town?'

'If I tell you where,' she whispered, bending closer, 'will you swear a terrible oath not to tell anybody?'

'I will.'

'Not even Florrie?'

'Not even Florrie.'

'That you might be killed stone dead?' she added in a blood-curdling tone.

'That I might be killed stone dead!'

'Well, there's a nice young man over from England who wants to marry me and bring me back with him. Of course, I said I couldn't come without you and he said he'd bring you as well . . . Wouldn't that be gorgeous?' she ended, clapping her hands.

' 'Twould,' said Terry, clapping his hands in imitation. 'Where's England?'

'Oh, a long way off,' she said, pointing up the valley. 'Beyond where the railway ends. We'd have to get a big boat to take us there.'

'Chrisht!' said Terry, repeating what Billy said whenever something occurred too great for his imagination to grasp, a fairly common event. He was afraid his aunt, like Mrs Early, would give him a wallop for it, but she only laughed. 'What sort of a place is England, Auntie?' he went on.

'Oh, a grand place,' said his aunt in her loud, enthusiastic way. 'The three of us would live in a big house of our own with lights that went off and on, and hot water in the taps, and every morning I'd take you to school on your bike.'

'Would I have a bike of my own?' Terry asked incredulously.

'You would, Terry, a two-wheeled one. And on a fine day like this we'd sit in the park – you know, a place like the garden of the big house where Billy works, with trees and flowers and a pond in the middle to sail boats in.'

'And would we have a park of our own, too?'

'Not our own; there'd be other people as well; boys and girls you could play with. And you could be sailing your boat and I'd be reading a book, and then we'd go back home to tea and I'd bath you and tell you a story in bed. Wouldn't it be massive, Terry?'

'What sort of story would you tell me?' he asked cautiously. 'Tell us one now.'

So she took off her black spectacles and, hugging her knees, told him the story of the Three Bears and was so carried away that she acted it, growling and wailing and creeping on all fours with her hair over her eyes till Terry screamed with fright and pleasure. She was really great gas.

Next day Florrie came to the cottage for him. Florrie lived in the village so she had to come a mile through the woods to see him, but she delighted in seeing him and Mrs Early encouraged her. 'Your young lady,' she called her and Florrie blushed with pleasure. Florrie lived with Miss Clancy in the post office and was very nicely behaved; everyone admitted that. She was tall and thin, with jet-black hair, a long ivory face, and a hook nose.

'Terry!' bawled Mrs Early. 'Your young lady is here for you,' and Terry came rushing from the back of the cottage with his new boat.

'Where did you get that, Terry?' Florrie asked, opening her eyes wide at the sight of it.

'My auntie,' said Terry. 'Isn't it grand?'

'I suppose 'tis all right,' said Florrie, showing her teeth in a smile which indicated that she thought him a bit of a baby for making so much of a toy boat.

Now, that was one great weakness in Florrie, and Terry regretted it, because he really was very fond of her. She was gentle, she was generous, she always took his part; she told creepy stories so well that she even frightened herself and was scared of going back through the woods alone, but she was jealous. Whenever she had anything, even if it was only a raggy doll, she made it out to be one of the seven wonders of the world, but let anyone else have a thing, no matter how valuable, and she pretended it didn't even interest her. It was the same now.

'Will you come up to the big house for a pennorth of goosegogs?' she asked.

'We'll go down the river with this one first,' insisted Terry, who knew he could always override her wishes when he chose.

'But these are grand goosegogs,' she said eagerly, and again you'd think no one in the world but herself could even have a gooseberry. 'They're that size. Miss Clancy gave me the penny.'

'We'll go down the river first,' Terry said cantankerously. 'Ah, boy, wait till you see this one sail – sssss!'

She gave in as she always did when Terry showed himself headstrong, and grumbled as she always did when she had given in. She said it would be too late; that Jerry, the under-gardener, who was their friend, would be gone and that Mr Scott, the head gardener, would only give them a handful, and not even ripe ones. She was terrible like that, an awful old worrier.

When they reached the riverbank they tied up their clothes and went in. The river was deep enough, and under the trees it ran beautifully clear over a complete pavement of small, brown, smoothly rounded stones. The current was swift, and the little sailing-boat was tossed on its side and spun dizzily round and round before it stuck in the bank. Florrie tired of this sport sooner than Terry did. She sat on the bank with her hands under her bottom, trailing her toes in the river, and looked at the boat with growing disillusionment.

'God knows, 'tisn't much of a thing to lose a pennorth of goosegogs over,' she said bitterly.

'What's wrong with it?' Terry asked indignantly. ' 'Tis a fine boat.'

'A wonder it wouldn't sail properly so,' she said with an accusing, schoolmarmish air.

'How could it when the water is too fast for it?' shouted Terry.

'That's a good one,' she retorted in pretended grown-up amusement. ' 'Tis the first time we ever heard of water being too fast for a boat.' That was another very aggravating thing about her – her calm assumption that only what she knew was knowledge. ' 'Tis only a cheap old boat.'

' 'Tisn't a cheap old boat,' Terry cried indignantly. 'My aunt gave it to me.'

'She never gives anyone anything only cheap old things,' Florrie replied with the coolness that always maddened other children. 'She gets them cost price in the shop where she works. Everyone knows that.'

'Because you're jealous,' he cried, throwing at her the taunt the village children threw whenever she enraged them with her supercilious airs.

'That's a good one too,' she said in a quiet voice, while her long thin face maintained its air of amusement. 'I suppose you'll tell us now what we're jealous of?'

'Because Auntie brings me things and no one ever brings you anything.'

'She's mad about you,' Florrie said ironically.

'She is mad about me.'

'A wonder she wouldn't bring you to live with her so.'

'She's going to,' said Terry, forgetting his promise in his rage and triumph.

'She is, I hear!' Florrie said mockingly. 'Who told you that?'

'She did; Auntie.'

'Don't mind her at all, little boy,' Florrie said severely. 'She lives with her mother, and her mother wouldn't let you live with her.'

'Well, she's not going to live with her any more,' Terry said, knowing he had the better of her at last. 'She's going to get married.'

'Who is she going to get married to?' Florrie asked casually, but Terry could see she was impressed.

'A man in England, and I'm going to live with them. So there!'

'A man in England?' Florrie repeated, and Terry saw he had really knocked the stuffing out of her this time. Florrie had no one to bring her to England, and the jealousy was driving her mad. 'And I suppose you're going?' she asked bitterly.

'I am going,' Terry said, wild with excitement to see her overthrown; the grand lady who for all her airs had no one to bring her to England with them. 'And I'm getting a bike of my own. So now!'

'Is that what she told you?' Florrie asked with a hatred and contempt that made him more furious still.

'She's going to, she's going to,' he shouted furiously.

'Ah, she's only codding you, little boy,' Florrie said contemptuously, splashing her long legs in the water while she continued to fix him with the same dark, evil, round-eyed look, exactly like a witch in a storybook. 'Why did she send you down here at all so?'

'She didn't send me,' Terry said, stooping to fling a handful of water in her face.

'But sure, I thought everyone knew that,' she said idly, merely averting her face slightly to avoid the splashes. 'She lets on to be your aunt but we all know she's your mother.'

'She isn't,' shrieked Terry. 'My mother is dead.'

'Ah, that's only what they always tell you,' Florrie replied quietly. 'That's what they told me too, but I knew it was lies. Your mother isn't dead at all, little boy. She got into trouble with a man and her mother made her send you down here to get rid of you. The whole village knows that.'

'God will kill you stone dead for a dirty liar, Florrie Clancy,' he said and then threw himself on her and began to pummel her with his little fat fists. But he hadn't the strength, and she merely pushed him off lightly and got up on the grassy bank, flushed and triumphant, pretending to smooth down the front of her dress.

'Don't be codding yourself that you're going to England at all, little boy,' she said reprovingly. 'Sure, who'd want you? Jesus knows I'm sorry for you,' she added with mock pity, 'and I'd like to do what I could for you, but you have no sense.'

Then she went off in the direction of the wood, turning once or twice to give him her strange stare. He glared after her and danced and shrieked with hysterical rage. He had no idea what she meant, but he felt that she had got the better of him after all. 'A big, bloody brute of nine,' he said, and then began to run through the woods to the cottage, sobbing. He knew that God would kill her for the lies she had told, but if God didn't, Mrs Early would. Mrs Early was pegging up clothes on the line and peered down at him sourly.

'What ails you now didn't ail you before?' she asked.

'Florrie Clancy was telling lies,' he shrieked, his fat face black with fury. 'Big bloody brute!'

'Botheration to you and Florrie Clancy!' said Mrs Early. 'Look at the cut of you! Come here till I wipe your nose.'

'She said my aunt wasn't my aunt at all,' he cried.

'She what?' Mrs Early asked incredulously.

'She said she was my mother – Auntie that gave me the boat,' he said through his tears.

'Aha,' Mrs Early said grimly, 'Let me catch her around here again and I'll toast her backside for her, and that's what she wants, the little vagabond! Whatever your mother might do, she was a decent woman, but the dear knows who that one is or where she came from.'

3

All the same it was a bad business for Terry. A very bad business! It is all very well having fights, but not when you're only five and live a mile away from the village, and there is nowhere for you to go but across the footbridge to the little railway station and the main road where you wouldn't see another kid once in a week. He'd have been very glad to make it up with Florrie, but she knew she had done wrong and that Mrs Early was only lying in wait for her to ask her what she meant.

And to make it worse, his aunt didn't come for months. When she did, she came unexpectedly and Terry had to change his clothes in a hurry because there was a car waiting for them at the station. The car made up to Terry for the disappointment (he had never been in a car before), and to crown it, they were going to the seaside, and his aunt had brought him a brand-new bucket and spade.

They crossed the river by the little wooden bridge and there in the yard of the station was a posh grey car and a tall man beside it whom Terry hadn't seen before. He was a posh-looking fellow, too, with a grey hat and a nice manner, but Terry didn't pay him much attention at first. He was too interested in the car.

'This is Mr Walker, Terry,' his aunt said in her loud way. 'Shake hands with him nicely.'

'How're ye, mister?' said Terry.

'But this fellow is a blooming boxer,' Mr Walker cried, letting on to be frightened of him. 'Do you box, young Samson?' he asked.

'I do not,' said Terry, scrambling into the back of the car and climbing up on the seat. 'Hey, mister, will we go through the village?' he added.

'What do you want to go through the village for?' asked Mr Walker.

'He wants to show off,' said his aunt with a chuckle. 'Don't you, Terry?'

'I do,' said Terry.

'Sound judge!' said Mr Walker, and they drove along the main road and up through the village street just as Mass was ending, and Terry, hurling himself from side to side, shouted to all the people he knew. First they gaped, then they laughed, finally they waved back. Terry kept shouting messages but they were lost in the noise and rush of the car. 'Billy! Billy!' he screamed when he saw Billy Early outside the church. 'This is my aunt's car. We're going for a spin. I have a bucket and spade.' Florrie was standing outside the post office with her hands behind her back. Full of magnanimity and self-importance, Terry gave her a special shout and his aunt leaned out and waved, but though Florrie looked up she let on not to recognise them. That was Florrie all out, jealous even of the car!

Terry had not seen the sea before, and it looked so queer that he decided it was probably England. It was a nice place enough but a bit on the draughty side. There were whitewashed houses all along the beach. His aunt undressed him and made him put on bright blue bathing-drawers, but when he felt the wind he shivered and sobbed and clasped himself despairingly under the armpits.

100

'Ah, wisha, don't be such a baby!' his aunt said crossly.

She and Mr Walker undressed too and led him by the hand to the edge of the water. His terror and misery subsided and he sat in a shallow place, letting the bright waves crumple on his shiny little belly. They were so like lemonade that he kept on tasting them, but they tasted salt. He decided that if this was England it was all right, though he would have preferred it with a park and a bicycle. There were other children making sandcastles and he decided to do the same, but after a while, to his great annoyance, Mr Walker came to help him. Terry couldn't see why, with all that sand, he wouldn't go and make castles of his own.

'Now we want a gate, don't we?' Mr Walker asked officiously.

'All right, all right, all right,' said Terry in disgust. 'Now, you go and play over there.'

'Wouldn't you like to have a daddy like me, Terry?' Mr Walker asked suddenly.

'I don't know,' replied Terry. 'I'll ask Auntie. That's the gate now.'

'I think you'd like it where I live,' said Mr Walker. 'We've much nicer places there.'

'Have you?' asked Terry with interest. 'What sort of places?'

'Oh, you know – roundabouts and swings and things like that.'

'And parks?' asked Terry.

'Yes, parks.'

'Will we go there now?' asked Terry eagerly.

'Well, we couldn't go there today; not without a boat. It's in England, you see; right at the other side of all that water.'

'Are you the man that's going to marry Auntie?' Terry asked, so flabbergasted that he lost his balance and fell.

'Now, who told you I was going to marry Auntie?' asked Mr Walker, who seemed astonished too.

'She did,' said Terry.

'Did she, by jove?' Mr Walker exclaimed with a laugh. 'Well, I think it might be a very good thing for all of us, yourself included. What else did she tell you?'

'That you'd buy me a bike,' said Terry promptly. 'Will you?'

'Sure thing,' Mr Walker said gravely. 'First thing we'll get when you come to live with me. Is that a bargain?'

'That's a bargain,' said Terry.

'Shake,' said Mr Walker, holding out his hand.

'Shake,' replied Terry, spitting on his own.

He was content with the idea of Mr Walker as a father. He

could see he'd make a good one. He had the right principles.

They had their tea on the strand and then got back late to the station. The little lamps were lit on the platform. At the other side of the valley the high hills were masked in dark trees and no light showed the position of the Earlys' cottage. Terry was tired; he didn't want to leave the car, and began to whine.

'Hurry up now, Terry,' his aunt said briskly as she lifted him out. 'Say night-night to Mr Walker.'

Terry stood in front of Mr Walker, who had got out before him, and then bowed his head.

'Aren't you going to say goodnight, old man?' Mr Walker asked in surprise.

Terry looked up at the reproach in his voice and then threw himself blindly about his knees and buried his face in his trousers. Mr Walker laughed and patted Terry's shoulder. His voice was quite different when he spoke again.

'Cheer up, Terry,' he said. 'We'll have good times yet.'

'Come along now, Terry,' his aunt said in a brisk official voice that terrified him.

'What's wrong, old man?' Mr Walker asked.

'I want to stay with you,' Terry whispered, beginning to sob. 'I don't want to stay here. I want to go back to England with you.'

'Want to come back to England with me, do you?' Mr Walker repeated. 'Well, I'm not going back tonight, Terry, but if you ask Auntie nicely we might manage it another day.'

'It's no use stuffing up the child with ideas like that,' she said sharply.

'You seem to have done that pretty well already,' Mr Walker said quietly. 'So you see, Terry, we can't manage it tonight. We must leave it for another day. Run along with Auntie now.'

'No, no, no,' Terry shrieked, trying to evade his aunt's arm. 'She only wants to get rid of me.'

'Now, who told you that wicked nonsense, Terry?' Mr Walker said severely.

'It's true, it's true,' said Terry. 'She's not my auntie. She's my mother.'

Even as he said it he knew it was dreadful. It was what Florrie Clancy said, and she hated his auntie. He knew it even more from the silence that fell on the other two. His aunt looked down at him and her look frightened him.

'Terry,' she said with a change of tone, 'you're to come with me at once and no more of this nonsense.'

'Let him to me,' Mr Walker said shortly. 'I'll find the place.'

She did so and at once Terry stopped kicking and whining and nosed his way into Mr Walker's shoulder. He knew the Englishman was for him. Besides he was very tired. He was half asleep already. When he heard Mr Walker's step on the planks of the wooden bridge he looked up and saw the dark hillside, hooded with pines, and the river like lead in the last light. He woke again in the little dark bedroom which he shared with Billy. He was sitting on Mr Walker's knee and Mr Walker was taking off his shoes.

'My bucket,' he sighed.

'Oh, by gum, lad,' Mr Walker said, 'I'd nearly forgotten your bucket.'

4

Every Sunday after, wet or fine, Terry found his way across the footbridge and the railway station to the main road. There was a pub there, and men came up from the valley and sat on the wall outside, waiting for the coast to be clear to slip in for a drink. In case there might be any danger of having to leave them behind, Terry brought his bucket and spade as well. You never knew when you'd need things like those. He sat at the foot of the wall near the men, where he could see the buses and cars coming from both directions. Sometimes a grey car like Mr Walker's appeared from around the corner and he waddled up the road towards it, but the driver's face was always a disappointment. In the evenings when the first buses were coming back he returned to the cottage and Mrs Early scolded him for moping and whining. He blamed himself a lot because all the trouble began when he broke his word to his aunt.

One Sunday, Florrie came up the main road from the village. She went past him slowly, waiting for him to speak to her, but he wouldn't. It was all her fault, really. Then she stopped and turned to speak to him. It was clear that she knew he'd be there and had come to see him and make it up.

'Is it anyone you're waiting for, Terry?' she asked.

'Never mind,' Terry replied rudely.

'Because if you're waiting for your aunt, she's not coming,' Florrie went on gently.

Another time Terry wouldn't have entered into conversation,

but now he felt so mystified that he would have spoken to anyone who could tell him what was keeping his aunt and Mr Walker. It was terrible to be only five, because nobody ever told you anything.

'How do you know?' he asked.

'Miss Clancy said it,' replied Florrie confidently. 'Miss Clancy knows everything. She hears it all in the post office. And the man with the grey car isn't coming either. He went back to England.'

Terry began to snivel softly. He had been afraid that Mr Walker wasn't really in earnest. Florrie drew closer to him and then sat on the grass bank beside him. She plucked a stalk and began to shred it in her lap.

'Why wouldn't you be said by me?' she asked reproachfully. 'You know I was always your girl and I wouldn't tell you a lie?'

'But why did Mr Walker go back to England?' he asked.

'Because your aunt wouldn't go with him.'

'She said she would.'

'Her mother wouldn't let her. He was married already. If she went with him he'd have brought you as well. You're lucky he didn't.'

'Why?'

'Because he was a Protestant,' Florrie said primly. 'Protestants have no proper religion like us.'

Terry did his best to grasp how having a proper religion made up to a fellow for the loss of a house with lights that went off and on, a park and a bicycle, but he realised he was too young. At five it was still too deep for him.

'But why doesn't Auntie come down like she always did?'

'Because she married another fellow and he wouldn't like it.'

'Why wouldn't he like it?'

'Because it wouldn't be right,' Florrie replied almost pityingly. 'Don't you see, the English fellow have no proper religion, so he wouldn't mind, but the fellow she married owns the shop she works in, and Miss Clancy says 'tis surprising he married her at all, and he wouldn't like her to be coming here to see you. She'll be having proper children now, you see.'

'Aren't we proper children?'

'Ah, no, we're not,' Florrie said despondently.

'What's wrong with us?'

That was a question that Florrie had often asked herself, but she was too proud to show a small boy like Terry that she hadn't discovered the answer.

'Everything,' she sighed.

'Florrie Clancy,' shouted one of the men outside the pub, 'what are you doing to that kid?'

'I'm doing nothing to him,' she replied in a scandalised tone, starting as though from a dream. 'He shouldn't be here by himself at all. He'll get run over . . . Come on home with me now, Terry,' she added, taking his hand.

'She said she'd bring me to England and give me a bike of my own,' Terry wailed as they crossed the tracks.

'She was only codding,' Florrie said confidently. Her tone changed gradually; it was becoming fuller, more scornful. 'She'll forget all about you when she has other kids. Miss Clancy says they're all the same. She says there isn't one of them worth bothering your head about, that they never think of anyone only themselves. She says my father has pots of money. If you were in with me I might marry you when you're a bit more grown-up.'

She led him up the short cut through the woods. The trees were turning all colours. Then she sat on the grass and sedately smoothed her frock about her knees.

'What are you crying for?' she asked reproachfully. 'It was all your fault. I was always your girl. Even Mrs Early said it. I always took your part when the others were against you. I wanted you not to be said by that old one and her promises, but you cared more for her and her old toys than you did for me. I told you what she was, but you wouldn't believe me, and now, look at you! If you'll swear to be always in with me I'll be your girl again. Will you?'

'I will,' said Terry.

She put her arms about him and he fell asleep, but she remained solemnly holding him, looking at him with detached and curious eyes. He was hers at last. There were no more rivals. She fell asleep too and did not notice the evening train go up the valley. It was all lit up. The evenings were drawing in.

PATRICK BOYLE
At Night All Cats Are Grey

Unwillingly he drifted up from sleep, burrowing deeper into the blankets, pulling around him the tattered fabric of his dream, clutching vainly at the urgent, embracing, anonymous arms that were slipping away into oblivion.

It was no use. The throbbing head, the parched and gritty palate drove him relentlessly awake. Soon nothing remained of the fierce demanding fingers tearing at his neck but an irritation below one ear.

He touched the spot. It was sore all right. Cautiously he explored elbows and knees. Nothing the matter there, thank God. Though it would be no surprise to find them bruised and cut. The whiskey that the publicans were dishing out these days was young enough to give you falling sickness. A few glasses and there you were – plunging around like a bee in a bottle. And, of course, the memory gone. Except for the inevitable glimpse of disaster. The close-up of a man's astonished face, streaked and frothed with porter. An uptilted shot of the underside of a lavatory cistern framed in what appeared to be the wooden seat of a W.C. The slow dissolve of a lower set of dentures grinning from a pool of puke. Just enough information to warn you of worse to come.

He rubbed his neck gently, trying to trace the outline of the injury. Barbed wire, perhaps? Or a thorn hedge? Could there have been a police raid on the last pub you were in? Maybe you were pushed out the back door, to stagger round blindly in the darkness, blundering against porter barrels, sheets of zinc, clothes-lines, empty bottles, in an effort to make a getaway? Were you caught? And questioned?

At this thought he squeezed his closed eyes tighter shut to damn up the flood of memories that might burst upon him.

It was all the fault of that wretched little mouse-about, Quigley – the curse of Christ on his hungry carcass. Serving up a bottle of stout that was no better than porter swill.

'Impossible to get the stout in condition this cold weather, Master James,' he whines, trying to raise a top on it by playing yo-yo with the bottle.

All because he's too mean to provide enough heat in his bar to condition the stout and warm his customers. By the time you've dealt with the flat, teeth-chattering brew you're just about ready to throw back a few whiskeys to warm your petrified stomach.

'A whiskey? I've a nice drop of Irish here. Ten year old. A large tumbler, as usual? And up to the top with aqua!'

When a publican elects to water your whiskey for you, it's time to watch out. But, of course, you know better. What matter if it smells like linoleum and tastes like first-run poteen? Drink enough of it and you don't notice. By closing time . . .

What time did you leave anyway? The last remembered sequence is of a foggy distorted Quigley mopping up the counter, from which all customers have, for some reason or other, retreated. Quigley is speaking but, due to faulty dubbing, the words do not synchronise with the movements of his mouth.

'That will be twelve shillings, Master James. And three shillings for the broken glasses.'

This scene, shot in blinding unforgettable Technicolour, ends abruptly with the sound of a heavy body falling.

After that, a jumble of vague impressions. A distant light, bobbing and swaying (a lantern?) in the darkness. A woman's voice (whose?) calling out: 'Who's there?' The loud ticking of a wag-o'-the-wall (in the name of God, where?). A hand (your own?) twisting the knob of a locked door.

What hell time did you get home last night? What shape were you in? Only one person could answer that. He ran a tongue round dry and tacky lips.

'Jeannie!' he called softly.

The shallow rapid breathing from the pillow beside him never faltered.

He turned over on his back, eyes still closed.

'Jeannie!' he called again. 'Are you awake?'

He reached out an exploratory, an appeasing hand, to ruffle gently the tangled mop of blonde silky hair. The breathing changed to a steady purr. It was that bloody Siamese ruffian, Wong!

Well, that was one mystery solved. The locked door. He must have got home so late that the wife had taken avoiding action. This must be the spare room he was in. Another spell of banish-

107

ment had commenced. And the ruddy cat had followed him into exile.

Obstinately he kept his eyes closed. What reason was there to open them anyway? The window would be in the usual place, looking out on the tiny cluttered yard. The birds had hardly migrated from the absurd and lurid wallpaper. The waxen-faced Christ, with scooped-out incandescent heart, would still stare down on him morosely from the far wall. On the mantelpiece the framed photograph of old Uncle Moneybags, singular vessel of devotion and long-awaited comforter of the afflicted, would still occupy the place of honour, though the old bastard will probably leave all his money to the Foreign Missions.

Did it really matter what time he was home last night? Or what time it was now? Or even what day, for that matter? There was no chance of change, even for the worse, in the monotony of his days. His life stretched out ahead of him – undeviating – settling deeper and ever deeper into the contented rut of happily married constancy. Gone for ever the hope of the unexpected, the certainty that round the very next corner lurks the fate that awaits you. Let it bring fear, delight, misery, enchantment – it is all one. The stimulus of change is what really matters.

Wong's purring had become intermittent. It was now laced with tiny sighs and moans. Shudders and twitchings racked his body as he sank back into sleep and, in shallow dream, stalked and killed, fought and rutted.

There was the life of Reilly! Owing no allegiance to anyone. Irresponsible. Receiving only gentle chidance for its sexual gluttony. Above all – discontented and disreputable.

The fog of second-rate contentment that fills this house . . . Ugh! You can hardly see out of the windows for the happiness clouding the glass. Like a bloody byre on a frosty night. Gum-chewing cows misting the air with their placid breath. Sweet-smelling dung-fragrant contentment! Small wonder a fellow would tear the coupon occasionally. Like yourself. Eh, Wong!

He reached out from under the clothes and stroked the unseen furry warmth. A burst of purring broke out. Sensuous claws were flexed on crinkling eiderdown.

Ha-ha, you blackguard! Are you getting notions? Pampering doesn't keep you at home either, does it?

At the sound of her step on the stairs, he pulled the clothes over his head and commenced breathing loudly and deeply. The door opened.

'Oh!' she said. 'Are you there too, Wong? Were you out on the tiles with His Lordship? You lucky males have all the fun.'

He heard her uncork the bottle.

'Two spoonfuls?' she asked.

He tried to breathe as sluggishly as possible.

'You're codding no one, you big baboon,' she said. 'Come out of hiding and take your liver salts.'

Spoon tinkled on glass. Fizzing sounds. He groaned.

'Sit up now, home-wrecker, before it goes flat.'

She tugged at the bedclothes.

Heaving himself up, he reached blindly for the glass. Why open his eyes? She would be standing there, a fond and stricken Madonna, oozing love and pity and anxiety. And soapy good health and sanity and main drainage and all the other Christian virtues. He heeled up the last of the salts and, gasping, sank back on the pillow, his nostrils still stinging with the spray.

'Hey, wait a minute!' she said, as he wriggled back under the clothes. 'Do I see lipstick?'

He groaned. Surely she didn't think he'd fall for *that* lure.

Throatily she growled:

'Who's been eating out of my bowl?'

Her breath fanned his cheek as she stooped to look. A moistened finger rubbed his neck.

'It's blood, you poor lamb! Were you in the wars again?'

He focused bleary eyes on her. Tall, slender, fair-skinned, blonde hair tucked into a scarf, she stood nervously twisting round her fingers the sash of her dressing-gown. Twisting the blade of remorse into his soul. It was so bloody unfair. She should have married a plaster saint and reared a plaster family somewhere in the Holy Land.

'Go away, Jeannie,' he said, 'and stop teasing me.'

'I'm not teasing you, Jim. I'm just trying to pretend I'm not worried.'

She soaked her handkerchief from the water carafe.

'I'll clean away the blood and see what it looks like,' she said.

Gently she dabbed at his injured neck.

'You know, darling, you frightened the life out of me last night. Kicking and battering the bedroom door. I thought you were going to burst it in. And the dreadful language. You were never like that before.'

He winced.

'Sorry, darling,' she said. 'The blood's badly caked.'

109

'I couldn't possibly have been as bad as you make out,' he said. 'I wasn't all that drunk.'

'And why do you lock the bedroom door anyway?' he said.

'It was and you were,' she said. 'And you know perfectly well I hate sleeping in an empty house. That's why I lock the door.'

'You should . . .'

'It was Wong!' she said triumphantly. 'Didn't I always tell you it was dangerous to have him in the bed?'

Bewildered, he rubbed his throbbing temples. He said:

'What on earth are you talking about, Jeannie?'

'The cat. Some time during the night you rolled over on Wong. And he scratched your neck. You're just lucky he didn't injure one of your eyes.'

As if he understood the conversation, the Siamese cat got up and, yawning, arched his back, stretched upwards on stiff bunched-together legs like the tentacles of a swimming jelly-fish. With tail erect and delicate grace he stalked, shaking the sleep from each paw as he went. At the bottom of the bed he stretched out, staring at them with disinterest from bleak blue eyes.

'Look at him!' she said. 'The picture of guilt.'

'The cat's not to blame, Jeannie. It was the floor of Quigley's barn. It reared up and bit me on the side of the head.'

She laughed.

'Poor lamb. Always the victim of circumstance.'

She pinched his cheek.

'You're a brute,' she said. 'A callous, cantankerous, guzzling brute. But you're the only brute I've got. So I must put up with you.'

Stooping, she kissed him and whispered against his closed lips:

'Get well, honey. Try to snap out of it.'

Desperately he floundered in the treacly flood that threatened to engulf him. His breathing quickened. The throbbing in his head took on a new, an urgent note. Weakly he pushed her away.

'I must smell like a sewer,' he said.

She pulled away, sniffing.

'Phew! Not exactly Chanel 5. Still, a hot bath and a good scrubbing out of your poor stomach-lining with Cascara and you'll be my sweet little baa-lamb again.'

He groaned.

'Beat it, will you?' he said.

She straightened up, grinning.

110

'Well, if it wasn't Wong scratched you, it was the claws of my hated rival.'

'Here!' she said, picking up a hand-mirror from the dressing-table. 'Look for yourself!' She thew it on the bed.

At the door, she turned. He was gazing into the mirror, a look of incredulity on his face.

She intoned softly:

> 'Mirror, mirror, on the wall,
> Who is the fairest of them all?'

Through the clink of the closing door she called:

'Don't go to sleep again, lazybones. I'm bringing up your breakfast directly.'

He heard nothing. He was staring at his scored neck. At the three parallel furrows reaching back from jawbone to God knows where on his neck. He screwed his head sideways but could not see where the scratches began.

These were never the claw-marks of a cat. They were much too far apart.

Painfully he tried to piece together the fragmented memories of last night. Had he really fallen in Quigley's? Could he have been in some sort of tussle? Did he stagger against anything on the way home? A fight or a fall would have left a permanent impression on his memory. Of that he was sure. Besides there would be tell-tale bruises.

No! It was something else.

Did he go straight home after leaving Quigley's? (He should have wormed out of Jeannie what time he had come home.) Could he have knocked up some other pub for more drink? Not impossible, but it rang no bell. What about a private house? Could he have staggered in somewhere on the way home and made a bloody nuisance of himself? Been flung out on his ear perhaps? Still no alarm bell.

Wait a moment! What was this nagging memory of a wag-o'-the-wall? Ticking away remorselessly. Where had he run into one of those antediluvian yokes? There weren't many of them around any more. But hold on now! Someone had spoken of one. With a bottle of water used as a driving weight. Regulated by the pouring out or in of a few drops of water. A real leery effort!

He put down the hand-mirror, closed his eyes and tried to concentrate.

Where in the village was there a bottle-driven clock? Patiently he put the question to the blob of colour floating across his eyelids. Like a pendulum it swung, drawn back and forth by his quivering jittery eyeballs. As the clock face began to take shape above the pendulum, he remembered.

Caroline, Jeannie's friend, had brought a wag-o'-the-wall recently at an auction.

Caroline Wentworth! Oh, God stone the crows! No matter how filthy rotten stinking drunk you were, you surely never burst in on the Wentworths – that pair of strait-laced, intolerant, sterilised snobs – to bore them with one of your open-confession-is-good-for-the-soul acts? Wallowing in your own filth so that Michael the Mealy-mouthed could punctuate your disclosures with dry censorious coughs and Caroline be given the opportunity of gazing at you with an expression of irony on her well-bred flawless features.

The images, flickering in vague merciful outline, sprang into focus. A long deserted street, in darkness but for a ground-floor light too many stumbling steps away. Towards this beacon you are making your way, groping along housewalls, doorways, windows, gateways. Bewildered when an entry or laneway sends you lurching into hollow darkness. Watching the solitary light grow nearer and brighter. Beckoning. It promises company. Talk, friendship, warmth, are at the core of its beam.

Then abreast of the window – halted. Listening. The wind, the river, the pounding blood, drowning out the murmuring voices. The fingernail tapping the glass – gently at first – but persisting until a woman's voice calls out: 'Who's there?'

Mewing impatiently, Wong prowled around the bed, padding across his motionless body, eventually coiling up once more on the pillow beside him. Abstractedly he stroked the bubbling throat, his thoughts swinging to the warm, lighted kitchen, the kettle purring on the range.

Caroline is making coffee. Very graceful in an ivory dressing-gown, dark hair gleaming, cheeks fire-flushed. As she moves around, telling in lowered voice of children lightly sleeping overhead: of Michael not yet back from the city; of the need to wait up for his return: of how glad she is to have company to shorten the night: of the sobering properties of coffee when taken piping hot: of Jeannie's kindness to her which could never, never be repaid.

The soft voice murmurs on, settling into the steady drone of the

112

Siamese who was now sprawled out, in abandon, across his chest. He lay on his belly, hind paws outstretched, a front paw shielding his eyes. Like a beckoning finger, the tip of his tail kept twitching spasmodically. At last it ceased and the purring dribbled into silence.

It is a silence with explosive qualities. Caroline is gazing at you oddly. As though something startling has been said. Her parted lips have surely this moment questioned: 'Why?' Or: 'Who?' Or even: 'Me?' Something must be done to shatter this perilous hush.

The halting tick of the wall-clock gives you your clue. Up with you on your feet. Finger pointing dramatically at the poor old wag that is just doing a job of work and minding its own business. 'There's the enemy! That bloody one-legged trickster! Ticking away like an arthritic old tortoise. But God help the hare that gets in its path. It'll get short shrift. It's no use, I tell you. It's too late.' Then, gripping the pendulum in one hand and the bottle-weight in the other: 'I've got a right to tear its guts out!'

All a lot of old hat. Angling for sympathy.

The next thing Caroline has jumped up. She is beside you whispering: 'Maybe it's not too late, Jim!' You stand facing each other with the click ticking away goodoh, until someone (who?) sways forward.

A sight for sore eyes, surely. The pair of you, locked in each other's arms, bolt upright in the middle of the kitchen floor, the lights full on, the children probably ear-wigging overhead, a scandalised Michael due to open the door any moment and Caroline . . .

Caroline clutching at you as if you were the last tattered fragment of a dream, slipping inexorably into oblivion. Caroline pleading: 'Don't, Jim, please! Please don't!' as if she really meant it. Caroline shivering as you slide a tentative hand along her smooth flanks. Caroline grinding her body against you and moaning: 'Darling! Darling! Darling!' Caroline's fingernails raking your neck before you manage to untangle yourself, soothing her with a promise . . .

'Did you go to sleep again, you loafer?'

Jeannie's voice, from the open door, startled him.

'And, good heavens, look at Wong! Get away, you treacherous brute!'

She pushed the Siamese roughly aside with the rim of the break-fast tray.

'He shouldn't be allowed up on the bed. Sit up straighter, Jim, or

113

you'll dribble tea on the bedclothes. It's a bad habit to give a cat.'

Wong, sprawled where he had fetched up, watched with cold, feral, unblinking eyes, as she settled the tray in place.

'That cat gives me the creeps. He looks at me as if I'm a mouse or a bird.'

She sat on the edge of the bed.

'How's your poor stomach, darling? I didn't do a fry. I thought tea and toast might be better. Don't take too long over it. You've only got an hour to go before Mass time. And you know how sharp Father John is. He hates people coming in late . . . '

Gingerly he swallowed a mouthful of orange juice and battled with his quaking stomach to keep it down. He closed his eyes. Jeannie's voice rippled on – soft, drowsy, meaningless.

'Beautiful day . . . sun splitting the trees . . . quick lunch . . . away early . . . golf date . . . Caroline . . . '

'Wha'sat?' he asked sharply, opening his eyes.

'You dozed off, you wretch. You didn't hear a word I said!'

'Sorry, Jeannie, I'm spun out about proper. More sleep's the only cure. What were you saying about golf?'

'Caroline and I are playing golf after lunch. Instead of wallowing in your bed, you should root out your clubs and come along.'

Racked by a violent fit of coughing, he put down his teacup. With streaming eyes and wheezing breath, he coughed and spluttered into his handkerchief.

'We shouldn't have too much trouble gathering up another male for a foursome. The bit of exercise would make a man of you. Was the tea too hot, dear?'

'I . . . I . . . I . . . ' He broke out coughing again.

'It's the same old excuse, I suppose. You're in bad form. Couldn't swing a club without your head bursting. But that's not the real reason. I know perfectly well what's wrong.'

Over the masking handkerchief his startled eyes queried her.

'You don't like Caroline. You think she's a snob. Well, she's not. She's just shy and quiet. Why don't you try to be nice to her? After all, she's my friend.'

Slowly he diced and buttered the fingers of toast. Without looking up, he said:

'I never thought I was anything else but nice to her.'

'You treat her as if she were some sort of a . . . what do you call that thing . . . that insect . . . that eats its husband?'

'The mantis,' he prompted. 'The praying mantis.'

'That's it. Like a praying mantis. That's how nice you are to her. And take that superior smile off your face, Mister Superman. You're going to treat her different from now on, or you'll have *me* to contend with.'

She glanced at her wrist and jumped up.

'Look at the time. We'll be late if we don't hurry.'

She rushed off, slamming the door. He heard her call from the head of the stairs:

'I'll run a bath for you and give a shout when it's ready.'

He pushed the breakfast tray to the side of the bed, grabbed up the Siamese and buried his face in the grassy fragrance of neck-fur.

'How's that for service, Wong?' he whispered.

He rolled the cat over on its back. Supine, it lay, paws outstretched, purring ecstatically while he tickled its belly.

'Things are beginning to pick up around here, Catty-puss. Eh?'

And indeed things were. The wallpaper was gay with flamingoes, pink and white absurdities, sleeping one-legged with heads wing-tucked: grazing in shallow water, spare sections of their hosepipe necks buckled inward: flying neck and legs outstretched, like exotic coathangers. From the wall, Christ smiled down on him indulgently. Uncle Moneybag's photograph seemed to promise the certainty of honourable mention in his last will and testament. The sunlit window opened up on a new world – a world of excitement, anxiety, intrigue, enchantment. A world of tip-and-run delight. Where desire prowls its path with breath sucked in and pounding heart. Where sleep is an enemy and daybreak disaster. A world of blanket-smothered coughs: of creaking bedsprings: of faces lit by pulsing cigarettes. A world of lies and cheating and fret and fear where love mushrooms up all-powerful only to creep away on stocking soles, parched and quivering.

Who would ever have thought that a few hours would have wrought such a change in his destiny? One moment faced with a lifetime of boring happiness: the next . . .

He stroked Wong's chops, flattening the cat's ears back, driving little squeaks of frenzy from its bared teeth.

'We'll have to make plans, Wong. Cunning, cat-like stratagems. What would you suggest, my friend?'

The first item on the agenda was to fill in last night's blank patches – where his mind had blacked out. Only Caroline could do that. It would require probing indeed to draw out significant memories without revealing that, for him, they had passed into oblivion. But it would have to be done. Without knowing where he had broken off, he would not know where to recommence.

But how to go about it? One false move and the delicate dream-like fabric of seduction would be ripped to tatters.

'Jim!' The call came faintly.

The Siamese was gnawing noisily at the pads of a hind paw. He pulled his head around gently by one ear.

'Did you hear that, Whiskers?' he said. 'There's the answer to our prayers.'

Jeannie! Of course! She was the solvent that would loosen Caroline's tongue. An evening spent in their company could well be a profitable one. After Jeannie's insistence on his being pleasant to her friend, she was hardly likely to suspect his sudden interest in Caroline and the innocent-seeming questions he would ply her with. And what woman, in the presence of the betrayed one, could resist the temptation of answering with the sly, ambiguous prattle of betrayal?

From the staircase well the call came again, louder:

'Jim!'

The cat cocked its ears, faced towards the door and made to rise.

'Stand your ground, gutless!' he said, flattening the struggling body against the counterpane. 'A little moral support, if you don't mind. We can pretend we're asleep. See!'

She was talking as she mounted the stairs:

'There's a poor way on a man when he's forced to talk to himself for lack of company. Though of course, if he's getting hard of hearing he mightn't know he's speaking out loud,' and opened the door:

'Don't tell me you didn't hear me. I called you often enough,' and stood by the bed:

'Is that wretched creature still here?' and tossed what felt like his dressing-gown across his length:

'Come on now, my old hunker-slider! Don't pretend you're sleeping. You tried that already this morning. Up you get! Your bath's drawn,' and lifted away the breakfast tray:

'If there's no harm in a lady asking, what's the significance of the smirk that's cracking your face in half,' and blew on his closed eyes until he was forced to open them:

'Out with it!' she said, grinning down at him. 'Whose saucer of milk did you lap up?'

She looked so vulnerable, so young and giddy and innocent, that the thought of betraying her was inconceivable. He said:

'I was just thinking I might make a few shillings of beer money by taking yourself and Caroline. A three-ball. Dollar a hole. And a dollar for dykes.'

'Would you concede a stroke a hole?'

'What do you think, Wong?' he said, running a finger gently up and down the cat's spine. 'Could we do it?'

The Siamese stretched out a paw and laid it delicately on his bare forearm. It was a gesture of trust and he was curiously moved by the pressure of the sponge-rubber pads. He continued to tickle the cat's spine whilst it squeaked and cried in slit-eyed ecstasy.

'We may take it that Wong thinks a stroke a hole reasonable,' he said.

'Perhaps we might have a meal somewhere afterwards. And a few drinks. Just the three of us,' he said.

She ruffled his hair.

'There are times, Jim, when you become almost human. Promise me only one thing and I'll sponsor you for husband of the year.'

'We know what she's after, don't we, pal?' he said, quickening the stroking pulse. 'We've not to guzzle more than two bottles of whiskey and a case of stout. Nor will we.'

Her hands fluttered in a small gesture of dismay.

'It's not that at all, darling. You can drink as much as you like. You know I never object. All I want you to do is to be nice to Caroline.'

His heart missed a beat. The stroking hand bore down convulsively on the cat's back.

Wong squealed. The velvet paw resting so innocently on his bare arm fanned out, claws exposed. With a swift movement it raked his arm from elbow to wrist.

'Jeeeesus!' he exclaimed, shoving the cat away roughly.

Still squealing and purring fervently, Wong retreated to the bottom of the bed where, with stiff legs and arched back, it danced ceremoniously on the bedclothes.

He stared at his scored arm in dismay. The three furrows, parallel and widely spaced, were just beginning to sprout blood. He watched as it spread, trickling through the hairs on his arm with little spurts like the zigzagging course of raindrops on a window pane.

'Oh, Jim, I told you so!' she wailed, grabbing up his handkerchief to staunch the blood. 'I warned you not to allow him in the bed. You know I did!'

He looked at her with eyes cold, implacable, sick with hatred.

'I told you so! I told you so!' he mimicked, in a cracked high-pitched voice.

He brushed her hand away. Wearily, bitterly, emphasising each word with upturned shaking head he told the stricken tallow-faced Christ:

'God almighty, how I loathe people who say: "I told you so!"'

MICHAEL McLAVERTY
The White Mare

'What about Paddy, Kate? He'll be raging if we let him lie any longer and it such a brave morning.'

'Och, let him rage away, Martha. He'll know his driver before night if he ploughs the field.'

''Deed that's the truth, and with an old mare that's done and dropping off her feet.'

'He'll get sense when it's too late. And to hear him gabbling you'd think he was a young man and not the spent old thorn that he is. But what's the use of talking! Give him a call.'

Kate, seated on a stool, blew at the fire with the bellows, blew until the flames were spurting madly in and out between the brown sods. Martha waited until the noise of the blazing fire had ceased, and then rapped loudly at the room door off the kitchen. The knocking was answered by a husky voice.

Paddy was awake, sitting up in the bed, scratching his head with his two hands and blinking at the bare window in the room. His face was bony and unshaven, his moustache grey and straggly. Presently he threw aside the blankets and crawled out backwards on to the cold cement floor. He stood at the window. In the early hours of the morning it had rained, but now it was clear. A high wind had combed the white hair of the sky, and on the bare thorn at the side of the byre shivered swollen buds of rain. Across the cobbled street was his stubble field, bounded on one side by a hedge and a hill, and on the other sides by loose stones. Two newly-ploughed furrows ran down the centre and at the top of them lay his plough with a crow swaying nervously on one of the handles. Last evening when the notion took him he had commenced the ploughing, and today, with the help of God, he'd finish it. He thought of the rough feel of the handles, the throb of the coulter cutting the clay, and the warm sweaty smell from his labouring mare.

With difficulty he stretched himself to his full height, his bony joints creaking, and his lungs filling with the rain-washed air that came through the open window; he drew in great breaths of it, savouring it as he would savour the water from a spring well. As he was about to turn away, the crow rose up suddenly and flew off. At that moment Kate was crossing to the byre, one hand holding a can, and the other a stick. Paddy watched, trying to guess from her movements the kind of temper she was in this morning. But he noted nothing unusual about her. There was the same active walk, the black triangle of shawl dipping down her back, and the grey head with the man's cap on it. To look at her you wouldn't think she was drawing the pension for over six years. No, there wasn't another house in the whole island with three drawing the pension – not another house! We're a great stock and no mistake; a great pity none of us married!

Kate's voice pierced the air as she shouted at a contrary cow. Oh, a good kind woman, but a tartar when you stirred her. He'd hold his tongue this morning till he had the mare tackled and then they could barge away. Anyway what do women know about a man's job, with their milking cows, and feeding hens, and washing clothes? H'm! a field has to be ploughed and it takes a man to plough it.

When he came from the room Kate was just in from milking and Martha moved slowly about the table arranging the mugs and the farls of bread. Paddy stooped and took his clay-caked boots from below the table. He knew by the look of his sisters that he'd have to lace them himself this morning. It always caused him pain to stoop, but what matter, he'd soon be out in the quiet of the fields where no one would say a word to him.

They all sat at the table together, eating silently and with the slow deliberation that comes with the passing years. Now and again as Paddy softened his bread in the tea, Kate would give him a hard little look. It was coming, he knew it. If only they'd keep silent until he had finished. But it was coming; the air was heavy with stifled talk.

'I suppose you'll do half the field today,' began Kate.

' 'Deed and I'll do it all,' he replied with a touch of hardness in his voice knowing he must be firm.

'Now, Paddy, you should get Jamesy's boys over to help you,' said Martha pleadingly.

'Them wee buttons of men! I'd have it done while they'd be thinkin' about it. I wouldn't have them about the place again, with their ordering this and ordering that, and their tea after their dinner, and wanting their pipes filled every minute with good tobacco. I can do it all myself with the help of God. All myself!' and with this he brought his mug down sharply on the table.

'If you get another attack of the pains it's us'll have to suffer,' put in Kate, 'attending you morning, noon and night. Have you lost your wits, man! It's too old you're getting, and it'd be better if we sold the mare and let the two bits of fields.'

Paddy kept silent; it was better to let them fire away.

'The mare's past her day,' Kate continued. 'It's rest the poor thing wants an' not pulling a plough with a done man behind it.'

'Done, is it? There's work in me yet, and I can turn a furrow as straight as anyone in the island. Done! H'm, I've my work to be doing.'

He got up, threw his coat across his shoulder, and strode towards the door. His two sisters watched him go out, nodding their heads. 'Ah, but that's a foolish, hard-headed man. There's no fool like an old fool!'

Paddy crossed to the stable and the mare nickered when she heard his foot on the cobbled street. Warm, hay-scented air met him as he opened the door. Against the wall stood the white mare. She cocked her ears and turned her head towards the light. She was big and fat with veins criss-crossing on her legs like dead ivy roots on the limbs of a tree. Her eyes were wet-shining and black, their upper lids fringed with long grey lashes. Paddy stroked her neck and ran his fingers through her yellow-grey mane.

A collar with the straw sticking out of it was soon buckled on, and with chains rattling from her sides he led her through the stone-slap into the field. He looked at the sky, at the sea with its patches of mist, and then smilingly went to his plough. Last evening, the coulter was cutting too deep and he now adjusted it, giving it a final smack with the spanner that rang out clear in the morning air. The mare was sniffing the rain-wet grass under the hedge and she raised her head jerkily as he approached, sending a shower of cold drops from the bushes down his neck. He shivered, but spoke kindly to the beast as he led her to be tackled. In a few minutes all was ready, and gripping the handles in God's name, he ordered the horse forward, and his day's work began.

The two sisters eyed him from the window. His back was towards them. Above the small stone fence they could see his bent figure, his navy-blue trousers with a brown patch on the seat of them, his grey shirt sleeves, the tattered back of his waistcoat, and above his shabby hat the swaying quarters of the mare.

'Did you ever see such a man since God made you! I declare to goodness he'll kill that mare,' said Martha.

'It's himself he'll kill if he's not careful. Let me bold Paddy be laid up after this and 'tis the last field he'll plough, for I'll sell the mare, done beast and all as she is!' replied Kate, pressing her face closer to the window.

Paddy was unaware of their talk. His eyes were on the sock as it slid slowly through the soft earth and pushed the gleaming furrows to the side. He was living his life. What call had he for help! Was it sit by and look at Jamesy's boys ploughing the field, and the plough wobbling to and fro like you'd think they were learning to ride a bicycle?

'Way up, girl,' he shouted to the mare, ' 'way up, Maggie!' and his veins swelled on his arms as he leant on the handles. The breeze blowing up from the sea, the cold smell of the broken clay, and the soft hizzing noise of the plough, all soothed his mind and stirred him to new life.

As the day advanced the sun rose higher, but there was little heat from it, and frosty vapours still lingered about the rock-heads and about the sparse hills. But slowly over the little field horse and plough still moved, moved like timeless creatures of the earth, while alongside their shadows followed on the clay. Over-head and behind swarmed the gulls, screeching and darting for the worms, their flitting shadows falling coolly on Paddy's neck and on the back of the mare. At the end of the ridge he stopped to take a rest, surveying with pleasure the number of turned fur-rows, and wondering if his sisters were proud of him now. He looked up at the house: it was low and whitewashed, one end thatched and the other corrugated. There seemed to be no life about it except the smoke from the chimney and a crow plucking at the thatch. Soon it flew off with a few straws hanging from its bill. It's a pity he hadn't the gun now, he'd soon stop that thief; at nestingtime they wouldn't leave a roof above your head. But tomorrow he'd fix them. He spat on his hands and gripped the handles.

At two o'clock he saw Kate making down at the top of the field and he moved to the hedge. She brought him a few empty sacks to sit on; a good kind girl when you took her the right way. She had the real stuff in the eggpunch, too, nothing like it for a working man.

When he had taken his first swig of tea she said quietly, 'It's time you were quitting, Paddy.'

122

He must be careful. 'Did you see that devil of a crow on the thatch?'

'I didn't, thank God. But I've heard it said that it's the sure sign of a death.'

'Did you now?' he replied with a smile. 'Isn't that queer, and me always thinking that it was the sign of new life and them nesting?'

It's no use trying to frighten him, she thought, no use talking to him; he'll learn his own lesson before morning. Up she got and went off.

'Give the mare a handful of hay and a bucket of water,' he called after her.

He lay back, smoking his pipe at his ease, enjoying the look of the ribbed field and the familiar scene. To his right over the stone fence lay the bony rocks stretching their lanky legs into the sea; and now and again he could hear the hard rattle of the pebbles being sucked into the gullet of the waves. Opposite on a jutting headland rose the white column of the East Lighthouse, as lonely-looking as ever. There never was much stir on this side of the island anyway. It was a mile or more from the quay where the little sailing boats went twice a week to Ballycastle. But what little there was of land was good. As he looked down at the moist clay, pressing nail-marks in it with his toe, he pitied the people in the Lower End with their shingly fields and stunted crops. How the news would travel to them tonight about his ploughing! Every mouthful of talk would be about him and the old white mare. He puffed at his pipe vigorously and a sweet smile came over his wrinkled face. Then the shouts of the children coming from school made him aware of the passing time.

He must get up now for the sun would set early. He knocked out his pipe on the heel of his boot. When he made to rise he felt stiff in the shoulders, and a needle of pain jagged one of his legs making him give a silly little laugh. It's a bad thing to sit too long and the day flying. He walked awkwardly over to Maggie, and presently they were going slowly over the field again. The yellow-green bands at each side of the dark clay grew narrower and narrower as each new furrow was turned. Soon they would disappear. The sky was clear and the sun falling; the daylight might hold till he had finished.

The coulter crunched on a piece of delph and its white chips were mosaiced on the clay. 'Man alive, but them's the careless women,' he said aloud. 'If the mare cut her feet there'd be a quare

123

how-d'y-do!' At that moment Kate came out to the stone fence and gathered clothes that had been drying. She stood with one hand on her cheek, looking at the slow, almost imperceptible, movement of the plough. She turned, shooshed the hens from her feet, and went in slamming the door behind her.

Over the rock heads the sun was setting, flushing the clay with gold, and burnishing the mould-board and the buckles on the horse. Two more furrows and the work was done. He paused for a rest, and straightened himself with difficulty. His back ached and his head throbbed, but what he saw was soothing. On the side of a hill his three sheep were haloed in gold and their long shadows sloped away from them. It was a grand sight, praise be to God, a grand sight! He bent to the plough again, his legs feeling thick and heavy. 'Go on, Maggie!' he ordered. 'Two more furrows and we're done.'

The words whipped him to a new effort and he became light with excitement. One by one the gulls flew off and the western sky burned red. A cold breeze sharp with the smell of salt breathed in the furrows. And then he was finished; the furrows as straight as loom-threads and not a bit of ground missed. A great piece of work, thanks be to God; a great bit of work for an old man and an old mare. He put on his coat and unyoked her. She felt light and airy as he led her by the head across the cobbles. Gently he took the collar from her, the hot vapour rising into the chilled air, and with a dry sack wiped her sides and legs and neck. A great worker; none better in the whole island. He stroked her between the ears and smiled at the way she coaxingly tossed her head. He put her in the stable; later on he'd be back with a bucket of warm mash.

It was semi-dark when he turned his back on the stable and saw the orange rectangle of light in the kitchen window. It was cold, and he shivered and shrugged his shoulders as he stood listening at the door.

In the kitchen it was warm and bright. The turf was piled high, and Martha and Kate sat on opposite sides of the hearth. Kate knitting and Martha peeling potatoes. He drew a chair to the fire and sat down between them in silence. The needles clicked rapidly, and now and then a potato plopped into the bucket. He must get out his pipe; a nice way to receive a man after a day's ploughing. The needles stopped clicking and Kate put her hands on her lap and stared at him from behind her silver-rimmed spectacles. Paddy took no notice as he went slowly on cutting his plug and grinding it between his palms. Then he spat in the fire, and Kate retorted by prodding the sods with her toe, sending sparks up the chimney. The spit hissed in the strained silence. The kettle sang and he rose to feed the mare.

'Just leave that kettle alone, Mister MacNeil,' said Martha.

'The mare has to be fed!'

'It's little you care about the poor dumb beast, and you out killing yourself and her, when it would suit you better to be in peeling these spuds.'

'It's little you do in the house but make the few bits of meals, and it's time you were stirring yourself and getting a hard-worked man a good supper.'

'If you're hard-worked, who's to blame, I ask you?' flared Kate.

He was done for now. He could always manage Martha; if he raised his voice it was the end of her. But Kate – he feared her though he wouldn't admit it to himself.

'Do you hear me, Paddy MacNeil? Who's to blame? Time and again we have told you to let the fields and have sense. But no; me bold boy must be up and leppin' about like a wild thing. And what'll the women in the island be talking about, I ask you? Ah! well we know what they'll be saying. "It's a shame that Paddy MacNeil's mean old sisters wouldn't hire a man to work the land. There they have poor Paddy and his seventy years, out in the cold of March ploughing with the old white mare. And the three of them getting the pension. I always knew there was a mean streak in them MacNeils." That's what they'll be saying, well we know it!'

'Talk sense, Kate, talk sense. Don't I know what they'll be saying. They'll be putting me up as an example to all and sundry. And . . .'

'But mark my words,' interrupted Kate, shaking a needle at him, 'if you're laid up after this you can attend to your pains yourself. I'm sick, sore and tired plastering and rubbing your shoulder and dancing attendance on you, and God knows I'm not able. I'm a done old woman myself, slaving from morning to night and little thanks I get for it.' Her voice quavered; crying she'll be next. It was best to keep silent.

'Get him his supper, Martha, till we get to bed – another day like this and I'm fit for nothing.' She lifted her hands from her lap and the needles clicked slowly, listlessly.

In silence he took his supper. He was getting tired of these rows. When he had finished he went out with a bucket of warm mash for the mare. He felt very weary and sleepy, but the cold night braced him a little. The moon was up and the cobbles shone blue-white like scales of a salmon. Maggie stirred when she heard the rasping handle of the bucket.

He closed the half-door of the stable, lit the candle, and sat on an upturned tub to watch the mare feeding. It was very still and she fed noisily, lifting her head now and again, the bran dripping from her mouth. Above the top of the door he could see the night-sky, the corrugated roof of the house, and the ash tree with its bare twigs shining in the moon. A little breeze blew its wavering pattern on the roof, and looking at it he thought of the gulls on the clay and the cool rush of their wings above his head. He shivered, and got up and closed the top half of the door. It was very still now; the mare had stopped feeding, her tail swished gently, and the warm hay glowed in the candlelight. There was great peace and comfort here. Under the closed door stole the night-wind, the bits of straw around the threshold rising gently and falling back again. A mouse came out from under the manger, rustled towards the bucket blinking its little eyes at the creature on the tub. Paddy squirted a spit at it and smiled at the way it raced off. He looked at the mare, watching the slight tremors passing down her limbs. He got up, stroked her silky neck and scratched her between the ears. Then he gave her fresh hay and went out.

It was very peaceful with the moon shining on the fields and the sea. He wondered if his sisters were in bed. He hesitated at the stone fence looking at the cold darkness of the field and the bits of broken crockery catching the moonlight. Through the night there came to him clear and distinct the throb, throb of a ship's engine far out at sea. He held his breath to listen to it and then he saw its two unsteady mastlights, rounding the headland and moving like stars through the darkness. It made him sad to look at it and he sighed as he turned towards the house. He sniffed the air like a spaniel; there'd be rain before long: it would do a world of good now that the field was ploughed.

His sisters were in bed; the lamp was lowered and the ashes stirred. He quenched the lamp and went up to his room. The moonlight shone in the window so he needn't bother with a candle. He knelt on a chair to say his prayers; he'd make them short tonight, for he was tired, very tired. But his people couldn't be left out. The prayers came slowly. His mind wandered. The

golden shaft of the lighthouse swept into the room, mysteriously
and quietly – light – dark – light – dark. For years he had watched
that light, and years after when he'd be dead and gone it would
still flash, and there'd be no son or daughter to say a prayer for
him. It's a stupid thing for a man not to get married and have
children to pray for him; a stupid thing indeed! It was strange to
be associating death with a lighthouse in the night, but in some
way that thought had come to him now that he was old, and he
knew that it would always come. He didn't stop to examine it.
He got up and sat on the chair, fumbling at his coat.

He climbed into bed, the straw mattress rustling with his weight.
He lay thinking of his day's work, waiting for sleep to fall upon
him. He closed his eyes, but somehow sleep wouldn't come. The
tiredness was wearing off him. He'd smoke for a while, that
would ease his mind. He was thinking too much; thinking kills
sleep. The moonlight left the room and it became oddly dark. He
stretched out his hand, groping for his pipe and matches. The
effort shot a pain through his legs and he stifled a groan. At the
other side of the wooden partition Kate and Martha heard him,
but didn't speak. They lay listening to his movements. Then they
heard the rasp of the match on the emery, heard him puffing at
the pipe, and saw in their minds its warm glow in the cold
darkness. There would be a long interval of silence, then the creak
of his bed, and another muffled groan.

'Do you hear him?' whispered Kate. 'We're going to have
another time of it with him. He has himself killed. But this is the
last of it!'

'He'll be harrowing the field next,' said Martha.

'Harrow he will not. Tomorrow, send a note to the horse-dealer
in Ballycastle.'

'Are you going to sell the mare, Kate?' Martha asked
incredulously.

'Indeed I am. There's no sense left in that man's head while
she's about.'

'Will you tell Paddy?'

'I'll tell him when she's sold, and that's time enough. So off
with the note first thing in the morning.'

A handful of rain scattered itself on the tin roof above their
heads. For a while there was silence, deep and dark and listening.
Then with a tree-like swish the rain fell, fell without ceasing, filling
the room with cold streaks of noise.

Paddy lay listening to its hard pattering. He thought of the broken field soaking in the rain, and the disturbed creatures seeking shelter under the sod, rushing about with weakly legs clambering for a new house, while down in the sea the fish would be hiding in its brown tangled lair disturbed by no plough. It's strange the difference between the creatures; all the strange work of God, the God that knows all. Louder and louder fell the rain. 'It's well the mare's in that night,' he said to himself, 'and it's well the field's ploughed.' He pictured the sheep pressing into the wet rocks for shelter, and the rabbits scuttling to their holes. Then he wondered if he had closed the stable door; it was foolish to think that way; he closed it, of course he closed it. His thoughts wouldn't lie still. The crow on the thatch flew into his mind. He'd see to that villain in the morning and put a few pickles in her tail. Some day he'd have the whole house corrugated. Maybe now the kitchen'd be flooded. He was about to get up, when the rain suddenly ceased. It eased his mind, and listening now to the drip-drop of water from the eaves, he slipped into sleep.

But in the morning he didn't get up. His shoulders, arms and legs were stiff and painful. Martha brought him his breakfast, and it was a very subdued man that she saw.

'Give me a lift up, Martha, on the pillows. That's a good girl. Aisy now, aisy!' he said in a slow, pained voice.

'Do you feel bad, Paddy?'

'Bravely, Martha, bravely. There's a wee pain across me shoulder, maybe you'd give it a rub. I'll be all right now when I get a rest.'

'You took too much out of yourself for one day.'

'I know, I know! But it'd take any other man three days to do the same field. Listen, Martha, put the mare out on the side of the hill; a canter round will do her a world of good.'

And so the first day wore on with his limbs aching, Martha coming to attend him, or Kate coming to counsel him. But from his bed he could see the mare clear as a white rock on the face of the hill, and it heartened him to watch her long tail busily swishing. On the bed beside him was his stick and on the floor a battered biscuit tin. Hour after hour he struck the tin with his stick when he wanted something – matches, tobacco, a drink, or his shoulder rubbed. And glad he was if Martha answered his knocking.

Two days passed in this way, and on the morning of the third the boat with the dealer was due. Time and again Martha went out on a hill at the back of the house, scanning the sea for the boat. At last she saw it and hurried to Kate with the news. Kate made a big bowl of warm punch and brought it to Paddy.

'How do you feel this morning?' she said when she entered the room.

'A lot aisier, thank God, a lot aisier.'

'Take this now and turn in and sleep. It'll do you good.'

Paddy took the warm bowl in his two hands, sipping slowly, and giving an odd cough as the strong whiskey caught his breath. Whenever he paused his eyes were on the window watching the mare on the hillside, and when he had finished, he sighed and lay back happily. His body felt deliciously warm and he smiled sweetly. Poor Kate; he misjudged her; she has a heart of corn and means well. Warm eddies of air flowed slowly through his head, stealing into every corner, filling him with a thoughtless ecstasy, and closing his eyes in sleep.

As he slept the dealer came, and the mare was sold. When he awakened he felt a queer emptiness in the room, as if something had been taken from it. Instinctively he turned to the window and looked out. The mare was nowhere to be seen and the stone-slap had been tumbled. He seized his stick and battered impatiently on the biscuit tin. He was about to get out of bed when Kate came into the room.

'The mare has got out of the field!'

'She has that and what's more she'll never set foot in it again.'

He waited, waited to hear the worst, that she was sick, or had broken a leg.

'The dealer was here an hour ago and I sold her, and, let me tell you, I got a pretty penny for her,' she added a little proudly.

His anger aroused him, and he stared at his sister, his eyes fiercely bright and his mouth open. Catching the rail of the bed he raised himself up and glared at her again.

'Lie down, Paddy, like a good man and quieten yourself. Sure we did it for your own good,' she said, trying to make light of it, and fixing the clothes up around his chest. 'What was she but a poor bit of a beast dying with age? And a good bargain we made.'

'Bargain, is it? And me after rearing her since she was a wee foal . . . No; he'll not get her, I tell you! He'll not get her!'

'For the love of God, man, have sense, have reason!'

But he wasn't listening. He brushed her aside with his arm, and his hands trembled as he put on his boots. He seized his stick and made for the door. They tried to stop him and he raised his stick to them. 'Don't meddle with me or I'll give you a belt with this!'

He was out, taking the short-cut down by the back of the house, across the hills that led to the quay. He might be in time; they'd hardly have her in the boat yet. Stones in the gaps fell with a crash behind him and he didn't stop to build them up, not caring where sheep strayed or cattle either. His eyes were fixed on the sea, on the mainland where Maggie was going. His heart hammered wildly, hammered with sharp stinging pains, and he had to halt to ease himself.

He thought of his beast, the poor beast that hated noise and fuss, standing nervously on the pier with a rope tied round her four legs. Gradually the rope would tighten, and she would topple with a thud on the uneven stones while the boys around would cheer. It was always a sight for the young, this shipping of beasts in the little sailing boats. The thought maddened him. His breath wheezed and he licked his dry, salty lips.

And soon he came on to the road that swept in a half circle to the quay. He saw the boat and an oar sticking over the side. He wouldn't have time to go round. Below him jutted a neck of rock near which the boat would pass on her journey out. He might be able to hail them.

He splashed his way through the shallow sea-pools on to the rock, scrambled over its mane of wet seaweed, until he reached the furthest point. Sweat was streaming below his hat and he trembled weakly as he saw the black nose of the boat coming towards him. He saw the curling froth below her bow. A large wave tilted the boat and he saw the white side of his mare, lying motionless between the beams. They were opposite him now, a hundred yards from him. He raised his stick and called, but he seemed to have lost his voice. He waved and called again, his voice sounding strange and weak. The man in the stern waved back as he would to a child. The boat passed the rock, leaving a wedge of calm water in her wake. The noise of the oars stopped and the sail filled in the breeze. For a long time he looked at the receding boat, his spirit draining from him. A wave washed up the rock, frothing at his feet, and he turned wearily away, going slowly back the road that led home.

BRYAN MacMAHON
The Ring

I should like you to have known my grandmother. She was my
mother's mother, and as I remember her she was a widow with a
warm farm in the Kickham country in Tipperary. Her land was on
the southern slope of a hill, and there it drank in the sun which, to
me, seemed always to be balanced on the teeth of the Galtees.
Each year I spent the great part of my summer holidays at my
grandmother's place. It was a great change for me to leave our
home in a bitter sea-coast village in Kerry and visit my grandmother's. Why, man, the grass gone to waste on a hundred yards
of the roadside in Tipperary was as much as you'd find in a
dozen of our sea-poisoned fields. I always thought it a pity to see
all that fine grass go to waste by the verge of the road. I still think
so.

Although my Uncle Con was married, my grandmother held
the whip hand in the farm. At the particular time I am trying to
recall, the first child was in the cradle. (Ah, how time has galloped
away! That child is now a nun in a convent on the Seychelles
Islands.) My Uncle Con's wife, my Aunt Annie, was a gentle,
delicate girl who was only charmed in herself to have somebody to
assume the responsibility of the place. Which was just as well
indeed, considering the nature of woman my grandmother was.
Since that time when her husband's horse had walked into the
farmyard unguided, with my grandfather, Martin Dermody, dead
in the body of the car, her heart had turned to stone in her breast.
Small wonder to that turning, since she was left with six young
children – five girls and one boy, my Uncle Con. But she faced the
world bravely and did well by them all. Ah! but she was hard, main
hard.

Once at a race-meeting I picked up a jockey's crop. When I
balanced it on my palm it reminded me of my grandmother. Once
I had a twenty-two pound salmon laced to sixteen feet of Castle-
connell greenheart; the rod reminded me of my grandmother.

131

True, like crop and rod, she had an element of flexibility, but like them there was no trace of fragility. Now after all these years I cannot recall her person clearly; to me she is something tall and dark and austere. But lately I see her character with a greater clarity. Now I understand things that puzzled me when I was a boy. Towards me she displayed a certain black affection. Oh, but I made her laugh warmly once. That was when I told her of the man who had stopped me on the road beyond the limekiln and asked me if I were a grandson of Martin Dermody. Inflating with a shy pride, I had told him that I was. He then gave me a shilling and said, 'Maybe you're called Martin after your grandfather?' 'No,' I said. 'I'm called Con after my Uncle Con.' It was then my grandmother had laughed a little warmly. But my Uncle Con caught me under the armpits, tousled my hair and said I was a clever Kerry rascal.

The solitary occasion on which I remember her to have shown emotion was remarkable. Maybe remarkable isn't the proper word; obscene would be closer to the mark. Obscene I would have thought of it then, had I known the meaning of the word. Today I think it merely pathetic.

How was it that it all started? Yes, there was I with my bare legs trailing from the heel of a loaded hay-float. I was watching the broad silver parallels we were leaving in the clean after-grass. My Uncle Con was standing in the front of the float guiding the mare. Drawing in the hay to the hayshed we were. Already we had a pillar and a half of the hayshed filled. My grandmother was up on the hay, forking the lighter trusses. The servant-boy was handling the heavier forkfuls. A neighbour was throwing it up to them.

When the float stopped at the hayshed I noticed that something was amiss. For one thing the man on the hay was idle, as indeed was the man on the ground. My grandmother was on the ground, looking at the hay with cold, calculating eyes. She turned to my Uncle Con.

'Draw in no more hay, Con,' she said. 'I've lost my wedding ring.'

'Where? In the hay?' he queried.

'Yes, in the hay.'

'But I thought you had a keeper?'

'I've lost the keeper, too. My hands are getting thin.'

'The story could be worse,' he commented.

My grandmother did not reply for a little while. She was eyeing the stack with enmity.

' 'Tis in that half-pillar,' she said at last. 'I must look for it.'

'You've a job before you, mother,' said Uncle Con.

She spoke to the servant-boy and the neighbour. 'Go down and shake out those couple of pikes at the end of the Bog Meadow,' she ordered. 'They're heating in the centre.'

'Can't we be drawing in to the idle pillar, mother?' my Uncle Con asked gently.

'No, Con,' she answered. 'I'll be putting the hay from the middle pillar there.'

The drawing-in was over for the day. That was about four o'clock in the afternoon. Before she tackled the half-pillar my grandmother went down on her hands and knees and started to search the loose hay in the idle pillar. She searched wisp by wisp, even sop by sop. My Uncle Con beckoned to me to come away. Anyway, we knew she'd stop at six o'clock. 'Six to six' was her motto for working hours. She never broke that rule.

That was a Monday evening. On Tuesday we offered to help – my Uncle Con and I. She was down on her knees when we asked her. 'No, no,' she said abruptly. Then, by way of explanation, when she saw that we were crestfallen: 'You see, if we didn't find it I'd be worried that ye didn't search as carefully as ye should, and I'd have no peace of mind until I had searched it all over again.' So she worked hard all day, breaking off only for her meals and stopping sharp at six o'clock.

By Wednesday evening she had made a fair gap in the hay but had found no ring. Now and again during the day we used to go down to see if she had had any success. She was very wan in the face when she stopped in the evening.

On Thursday morning her face was still more strained and drawn. She seemed reluctant to leave the rick even to take her meals. What little she ate seemed like so much dust in her mouth. We took down tea to her several times during the day.

By Friday the house was on edge. My Uncle Con spoke guardedly to her at dinner-time. 'This will set us back a graydle, mother,' he said. 'I know, son; I know, son; I know,' was all she said in reply.

Saturday came and the strain was unendurable. About three o'clock in the afternoon she found the keeper. We had been watching her in turns from the kitchen window. I remember my uncle's face lighting up and his saying, 'Glory, she's found it!' But he drew a long breath when again she started burrowing feverishly in the hay. Then we knew it was only the keeper. We didn't run out at all. We waited till she came in at six o'clock. There were times between three and six when our three heads were together at the small window watching her. I was thinking she was like a mouse nibbling at a giant's loaf.

At six she came in and said, 'I found the keeper.' After her tea she couldn't stay still. She fidgeted around the kitchen for an hour or so. Then, 'Laws were made to be broken,' said my grandmother with a brittle bravery, and she stalked out to the hayshed. Again we watched her.

Coming on for dusk she returned and lighted a stable lantern and went back to resume her search. Nobody crossed her. We didn't say yes, aye or no to her. After a time my Uncle Con took her heavy coat off the rack and went down and threw it across her shoulders. I was with him. 'There's a touch of frost there to-night, mother,' said my Uncle Con.

We loitered for a while in the darkness outside the ring of her lantern's light. But she resented our pitying eyes so we went in. We sat around the big fire waiting – Uncle Con, Aunt Annie and I. That was the lonely waiting – without speaking – just as if we were waiting for an old person to die or for a child to come into the world. Near twelve we heard her step on the cobbles. 'Twas typical of my grandmother that she placed the lantern on the ledge of the dresser and quenched the candle in it before she spoke to us.

'I found it,' she said. The words dropped out of her drawn face.

'Get hot milk for my mother, Annie,' said Uncle Con briskly.

My grandmother sat by the fire, a little to one side. Her face was as cold as death. I kept watching her like a hawk but her eyes didn't even flicker. The wedding ring was inside its keeper, and my grandmother kept twirling it round and round with the fingers of her right hand.

Suddenly, as if ashamed of her fingers' betrayal, she hid her hands under her check apron. Then, unpredictably, the fists under the apron came up to meet her face, and her face bent down to meet the fists in the apron. 'Oh, Martin, Martin,' she sobbed, and then she cried like the rain.

ANTHONY C. WEST
Not Isaac

Stephen Muir's father and the three men on the farm always considered that the boy was soft, especially about killing things. They often joked him, hoping to stiffen him, but only enraging him because he could not explain what he felt about taking an animal's life.

When he crossed sixteen the matter came to a head. And that autumn, when a large pig was being slaughtered for the domestic bacon supply, his softness was clearly demonstrated to all, save his gentle mother.

The three men – Bill Brady, John Conlan and Tommie Maguire – had driven the hog into an enclosed yard where it innocently nosed about, having had nothing but rough care and food from human beings till then. Two of the men had heavy sticks and Brady, a sort of untitled foreman, was armed with a seven-pound sledgehammer. He walked quietly up to the animal, measured it, set himself, and swung the hammer, intending to hit the beast squarely between the eyes and stun it till the throat could be slit.

But the pig moved its head slightly and took the blow on an ear. It fell, struggled, Brady roaring at the others to help him hold it down, Stephen knowing they were half scared of it. The beast got up. throwing the three men off, and staggered round in crazy circles, now knowing enough to mistrust completely Brady and his hammer. Falling and rising and shaking its head as if to dislodge the pain, it squealed in terror each time any of them approached it. Brady was annoyed and the others started to laugh hysterically.

Brady chased after it, the hammer ready for a more damaging blow. They united to drive it into a corner, but the animal seemed to have realised that corners were fatal things and, in spite of the urgent shouts and blows, it persisted in staggering wantonly about the middle of the yard.

Brady lost his temper completely and tried to deliver several

135

random blows as the pig dodged about. One swipe struck the nose and another gashed the sound ear.

Stephen had been watching all this from an upstairs window. Normally, he never interfered with the men and the fact that he was his father's son gave him no authority over them. He felt Brady's hammer blows on his own head and desperately tried to think of a way to help the animal into an easier, quicker death.

Both parents were out and old Tilly Magee, the cook-cum-housekeeper, was deaf as an old oak post. Then he remembered that his father had a small old-fashioned revolver in a cupboard. He had often played with the weapon and knew how to use it even if he had never fired a shot.

He found the gun and one ancient shell and ran out with it to the yard. The maimed and bloody pig was snorting in fear and blindly seeking impossible escape, the three men now beside themselves with frustrated, tense rage, their three simple minds locked to the animal as if it must die so that they might continue to exist.

They paid no heed to the boy at first and he had to shout and hold Brady's coat before the man desisted in the crazy chase. He was so full of rage of a different kind that the tears came to his eyes.

The men stopped, self-consciously, their three pairs of eyes staring and bloodshot and, like the pig, breathing stertorously through open, frothy mouths, their lips mauve with anger and exertion. Brady swore coarsely at the animal as if it were at fault for not going quietly to death.

Stephen slipped the shell into the correct chamber in the gun, handing it to Brady and telling him to hold the barrel close to the pig's head. Then he went away quickly and very soon heard the shot. From the window he saw them hurrying from the boiler house with pails of steaming water and knew that the selfless gun had done its duty.

Afterwards, the men probably felt embarrassed about the affair and to cover up they joked the boy more heavily as if their ferine brutality was all of manhood and Stephen's pale face and tears were weak and womanish. Conor Muir was ashamed of his son's apparent lack of pluck, taking it almost as a personal slight on blood and country breeding, as if the boy had stolen something or in some way had brought ill repute upon the house. And he bawled Stephen out for interfering with the old gun, saying it might have blown off Brady's hand.

Stephen said nothing about the pig. His father would have been angry, not in sympathy with the animal, but because the manhandling might have damaged the bacon.

Brady was Stephen's most articulate tormentor; he had an acrid wit and some self-importance. Conlan was his half-brother and Maguire was his cousin. As their fathers before them, they had worked on the farm since boyhood. The three of them were very alike. They had thick, strong bodies, heavy, red necks, long noses with hairy slits for nostrils, and high, narrow heads. Essentially they were brutal. Their lives had asked them for little learning or finesse. To them, as to Conor Muir, a cow was a thing on four legs with an udder for milk between the two hind ones and worth so many pounds.

Finally, to silence and satisfy everyone, Stephen volunteered to kill and dress the Christmas wether, which was always divided fairly between the Muirs and the men for the holiday. The event was to take place on the first wet afternoon of Christmas week as they had been busy with autumn cultivations made late by a stormy November.

For days the weather remained bright and dry and Stephen remembered looking for each sunrise and wishing the day would continue fine. He knew the gentle beast he was to slay. He could remember it as a curly, playful lamb. It was running with half a dozen others in a small field behind the barn. They all had the white face and high nose of the Cheviot and were pathetically harmless and inoffensive. Always they bunched together in the far corner of the field when anyone came to the gate; standing and gazing curiously and nodding their heads, not exactly in fear, but in generic nervousness. When one moved they all moved, seeming to abhor solitariness or isolation.

On the Thursday, four days before Christmas, rain fell all day and at lunch-time Conor Muir said the sheep would be killed. His wife said nothing, looking down at her plate and covertly glancing at her son with a gleam of sympathy in her grey eyes.

After the meal Stephen saw Brady sloping down the fields with the dog, a sack over his shoulders to break the rain and puttees of sacking wrapped around his legs. He seemed to move with overt cockiness as if in anticipation of a diversion.

Stephen went to the old larder with its high racks of wicked hooks from ceiling to floor, reminding him of tales about medieval torture chambers. Even as a child he had always hated the place with its hooks and smells as if the ghosts of the animals it had seen slaughtered had haunted it.

Conlan and Maguire were waiting for the wether to come, smoking their rank pipes and spreading odours of wet, cow-smelling clothes. As Stephen took off his jacket Conlan asked him how he felt, winking at his cousin. Stephen did not answer and took up the little sticking knife and commenced to sharpen it on the steel.

Whet-whet! Whet-whet! the steel said to the knife's unseen edge almost like a bird call. There was a low, strong table like a butcher's block, slightly cupped and black in the cracks with old blood, and the whole larder smelled slightly of rancid grease and carbolic.

They heard the dog bark and the chopping patter of the wether's nervous hoofs. The collie rushed past the beast, turning it back and holding it for Brady to drive into the small walled yard outside the larder door. Conlan and Maguire went out while Stephen waited, his mind now becoming dull and registering every move in slow motion.

There was a slight scuffle over the rain sounds on the roof as the sheep was caught and someone swore at the excited dog, telling it to go and lie down. Then the three men dragged in the victim, one at each shoulder and one at its rump, their big red hands buried deeply in the grey-white fleece. The wether did not bleat or struggle and only slid along the tiled floor on four stiff legs.

Stephen held the knife behind his back, ashamed to let the little animal see it, Abraham and thickets and ancient sacrifices running through his mind. As if the knife itself had bid him he felt his hand tighten on the haft.

The sheep panted with short silent pants, the slitted nostrils moving as the gills of a fish. And its head, its lovely antique head, was wise and beautiful with a terrible and uncomplaining wisdom aware of a long past through which its race had furnished food for knives, bellies, and altars and had heard the sonorous names of long-forgotten gods chanted in gloomy cave, tumulus, and lavish temple.

And its eyes were there, not seeing him nor knife more than another thing. That was the terrible part of it – the virgin, fearless, guiltless innocence. But still he held the knife, the blade against his wrist, for the eyes were grey with kindess, sleepy, and barred with long jewelled stones of beauty snared in honest opal fire.

'Up on the bench with her!' Brady was saying.

They lifted it with unnecessary roughness on to the block. It lay awkwardly on its side, the four very neat legs struck out, the neck and head thrown back as if in fatalistic readiness. It struggled a little and they held it down. It did not struggle against fear or hurt or death, but because it was uncomfortable.

Stephen's hand slowly bared the dull fang of knife and he looked down on it. Harlot it was to any man's hand; a cruel, strong thing not made for kindness and healing . . .

'Come on, me boy!' Maguire urged. 'What are ye waitin' for?'

The others laughed. Stephen looked up at them, balancing the knife in his hand, and he could only see three beings holding a fourth down.

Reaching forward his left hand he grasped the beast's satin throat, feeling for the windpipe, then edging his fingers back to the ear, his right hand hardening on the knife haft. Poising the blade just behind the jaw-root, he pressed firmly down without resistance.

The barred eye never changed nor challenged, showing neither fear nor blame. Nor did the body struggle against the mortal wounding. With rigid forearm he pressed the knife home, turning it and outcutting invisibly.

And still the beauty of the eye remained unchanged. Slowly the breathing weakened and blood snored in the lungs, the bright breath-blood dripping slowly from the twitching nostrils with astonishing brightness while the limbs impulsively protested a very little as a worm might curl when a spade touches it.

Stephen withdrew the knife, looking at it curiously, its moist, senseless blade having partaken of a mystery greater than any man might bear, and he was thinking whimsically it was a poor repayment for that first innocent witness so long ago when the barred eyes had gazed on beauty on a mother's knee, their body heat keeping the stable warm.

'Come on! Off with her skin!' Brady was goading, still looking slyly at the others. They had agreed between themselves not to help him, but he knew exactly what to do.

And for him now, the killing over, the beast was no more than an unfashioned stone or lump of unshaped clay.

But his hand was still hard on the knife and sheep smell oozed over his face as he wiped the sweat off with the back of his left hand. The knife, locked rigid his forearm and he saw three similar throats, red-necked and slightly hairy with their protruding

139

Adam's apples, arrogant and ignorant, in minds subhuman and human only in form. And he saw three pairs of guileful eyes half-smiling at his lividness and still the ready knife held fast his hand, still poised, greedy, insatiable, tireless.

He turned to the sheep as it moved comfortably and sighed contentedly, the eye still barred in beauty's harmless death. Without direction from Brady, he flayed the carcass and they helped him hang it, then watched him paunch it. Gently the soft grey guts slipped out of the gaping belly-slit, pathetic in the indecent exposure, and still pulsing in their peristaltic action. The birthed, skinless form mightily like a man's pink, marble-fatted flesh – Death? No. No longer sheep, no longer anything.

For their benefit he even decorated the flanks with little cuts that made an ash-leaf pattern on the warm elastic flesh.

When he finished they were full of praise. Suddenly he turned on them, holding the knife blade between his right finger and thumb. Then slowly he raised his arm and flung it with all his strength at the door, the point going deeply, gladly, into the wood and shivering as with life.

Then he took his jacket and walked out quietly into the soft clean evening on which the rain had ceased to fall and a thrush was singing gaily in the sycamore tree over the larder roof in faithful anticipation of the spring.

MARY LAVIN
Happiness

Mother had a lot to say. This does not mean she was always talking but that we children felt the wells she drew upon were deep, deep, deep. Her theme was happiness: what it was, what it was not; where we might find it, where not; and how, if found, it must be guarded. Never must we confound it with pleasure. Nor think sorrow its exact opposite.

'Take Father Hugh.' Mother's eyes flashed as she looked at him. 'According to him, sorrow is an ingredient of happiness – a *necessary* ingredient, if you please!' And when he tried to protest she put up her hand. 'There may be a freakish truth in the theory - – for some people. But not for me. And not, I hope, for my children.' She looked severely at us three girls. We laughed. None of us had had much experience with sorrow. Bea and I were children and Linda only a year old when our father died suddenly after a short illness that had not at first seemed serious. 'I've known people to make sorrow a *substitute* for happiness,' Mother said.

Father Hugh protested again. 'You're not putting me in that class, I hope?'

Father Hugh, ever since our father died, had been the closest of anyone to us as a family, without being close to any one of us in particular – even to Mother. He lived in a monastery near our farm in County Meath, and he had been one of the celebrants at the Requiem High Mass our father's political importance had demanded. He met us that day for the first time, but he took to dropping in to see us, with the idea of filling the crater of loneliness left at our centre. He did not know that there was a cavity in his own life, much less that we would fill it. He and Mother were both young in those days and perhaps it gave scandal to some that he was so often in our house, staying till late into the night and, indeed, thinking nothing of stopping all night if there was any special reason, such as one of us being sick. He had even on

141

occasion slept there if the night was too wet for tramping home across the fields.

When we girls were young, we were so used to having Father Hugh around that we never stood on ceremony with him but in his presence dried our hair and pared our nails and never minded what garments were strewn about. As for Mother – she thought nothing of running out of the bathroom in her slip, brushing her teeth or combing her hair, if she wanted to tell him something she might otherwise forget. And she brooked no criticism of her behaviour. 'Celibacy was never meant to take all the warmth and homeliness out of their lives,' she said.

On this point, too, Bea was adamant. Bea, the middle sister, was our oracle. 'I'm so glad he *has* Mother,' she said, 'as well as her having him, because it must be awful the way most women treat them – priests, I mean – as if they were pariahs. Mother treats him like a human being – that's all!'

And when it came to Mother's ears that there had been gossip about her making free with Father Hugh, she opened her eyes wide in astonishment. 'But he's only a priest!' she said.

Bea giggled. 'It's a good job he didn't hear *that*,' she said to me afterwards. 'It would undo the good she's done him. You'd think he was a eunuch.'

'Bea!' I said. 'Do you think he's in love with her?'

'If so, he doesn't know it,' Bea said firmly. 'It's her soul he's after. Maybe he wants to make sure of her in the next world!'

But thoughts of the world to come never troubled Mother. 'If anything ever happens to me, children,' she said, 'suddenly, I mean, or when you are not near me, or I cannot speak to you, I want you to promise you won't feel bad. There's no need! Just remember that I had a happy life – and that if I had to choose my kind of heaven I'd take it on this earth with you again, no matter how much you might annoy me!'

You see, annoyance and fatigue, according to Mother, and even illness and pain, could coexist with happiness. She had a habit of asking people if they were happy at times and in places that – to say the least of it – seemed to us inappropriate. 'But are you happy?' she'd probe as one lay sick and bathed in sweat, or in the throes of a jumping toothache. And once in our presence she made the inquiry of an old friend as he lay upon his deathbed.

'Why not?' she said when we took her to task for it later. 'Isn't it more important than ever to be happy when you're dying? Take my own father! You know what he said in his last moments? On

142

his deathbed, he defied me to name a man who had enjoyed a better life. In spite of dreadful pain, his face *radiated* happiness!' Mother nodded her head comfortably. 'Happiness drives out the pain, as fire burns out fire.'

Having no knowledge of our own to pit against hers, we thirstily drank in her rhetoric. Only Bea was sceptical. 'Perhaps you *got* it from him, like spots, or fever,' she said. 'Or something that could at least be slipped from hand to hand.'

'Do you think I'd have taken it if that were the case!' Mother cried. 'Then, when he needed it most?'

'Not there and then!' Bea said stubbornly. 'I meant as a sort of legacy.'

'Don't you think in *that* case,' Mother said, exasperated, 'he would have felt obliged to leave it to your grandmother?'

Certainly we knew that in spite of his lavish heart our grandfather had failed to provide our grandmother with enduring happiness. He had passed that job on to Mother. And Mother had not made too good a fist of it, even when Father was living and she had him – and, later, us children – to help.

As for Father Hugh, he had given our grandmother up early in the game. 'God Almighty couldn't make that woman happy,' he said one day, seeing Mother's face, drawn and pale with fatigue, preparing for the nightly run over to her own mother's flat that would exhaust her utterly.

There were evenings after she came home from the library where she worked when we saw her stand with the car keys in her hand, trying to think which would be worse – to slog over there on foot, or take out the car again. And yet the distance was short. It was Mother's day that had been too long.

'Weren't you over to see her this morning?' Father Hugh demanded.

'No matter!' said Mother. She was no doubt thinking of the forlorn face our grandmother always put on when she was leaving. ('Don't say good night, Vera,' Grandmother would plead. 'It makes me feel too lonely. And you never can tell – you might slip over again before you go to bed!')

'Do you know the time?' Bea would say impatiently, if she happened to be with Mother. Not indeed that the lateness of the hour counted for anything, because in all likelihood Mother *would* go back, if only to pass by under the window and see that the lights were out, or stand and listen and make sure that as far as she could tell all was well.

143

'I wouldn't mind if she was happy,' Mother said.

'And how do you know she's not?' we'd ask.

'When people are happy, I can feel it. Can't you?'

We were not sure. Most people thought our grandmother was a gay creature, a small birdy being who even at a great age laughed like a girl, and – more remarkably – sang like one, as she went about her day. But beak and claw were of steel. She'd think nothing of sending Mother back to a shop three times if her errands were not exactly right. 'Not sugar like that – that's *too* fine; it's not castor sugar I want. But *not* as coarse as *that*, either. I want an in-between kind.'

Provoked one day, my youngest sister, Linda, turned and gave battle. 'You're mean!' she cried. 'You love ordering people about!'

Grandmother preened, as if Linda had acclaimed an attribute. 'I was always hard to please,' she said. 'As a girl, I used to be called Miss Imperious.'

And Miss Imperious she remained as long as she lived, even when she was a great age. Her orders were then given a wry twist by the fact that as she advanced in age she took to calling her daughter Mother, as we did.

There was one great phrase with which our grandmother opened every sentence: 'if only'. 'If only,' she'd say, when we came to visit her – 'if only you'd come earlier, before I was worn out expecting you!' Or if we were early, then if only it was later, after she'd had a rest and could enjoy us, be *able* for us. And if we brought her flowers, she'd sigh to think that if only we'd brought them on the previous day she'd have had a visitor to appreciate them, or say it was a pity the stems weren't longer. If only we'd picked a few green leaves, or included some buds, because, she said disparagingly, the poor flowers we'd brought were already wilting. We might just as well not have brought them! As the years went on, Grandmother had a new bead to add to her rosary: if only her friends were not all dead! By their absence, they reduced to nil all *real* enjoyment in anything. Our own father – her son-in-law – was the one person who had ever gone close to pleasing her. But even here there had been a snag. 'If only he was my real son!' she used to say, with a sigh.

Mother's mother lived on through our childhood and into our early maturity (though she outlived the money our grandfather left her), and in our minds she was a complicated mixture of valiance and defeat. Courageous and generous within the limits of her own life, her simplest demand was yet enormous in the larger frame of Mother's life, and so we never could see her with the same clarity of vision with which we saw our grandfather, or our own father. Them we saw only through Mother's eyes.

'Take your grandfather!' she'd cry, and instantly we'd see him, his eyes burning upon us – yes, upon *us,* although in his day only one of us had been born: me. At another time, Mother would cry, 'Take your own father!' and instantly we'd see *him* – tall, handsome, young, and much more suited to marry one of us than poor bedraggled Mother.

Most fascinating of all were the times Mother would say, 'Take me!' By magic then, staring down the years, we'd see blazingly clear a small girl with black hair and buttoned boots, who, though plain and pouting, burned bright, like a star. 'I was happy, you see,' Mother said. And we'd strain hard to try and understand the mystery of the light that still radiated from her. 'I used to lean along a tree that grew out over the river,' she said, 'and look down through the grey leaves at the water flowing past below, and I used to think it was not the stream that flowed but me, spreadeagled over it, who flew through the air! Like a bird! That I'd found the secret!' She made it seem there might *be* such a secret, just waiting to be found.

Another time she'd dream that she'd be a great singer.

'We didn't know you sang, Mother!'

She had to laugh. 'Like a crow,' she said.

Sometimes she used to think she'd swim the Channel.

'Did you swim *that* well, Mother?'

'Oh, not really – just the breast stroke,' she said. 'And then only by the aid of two pig bladders blown up by my father and tied around my middle. But I used to throb – yes, throb – with happiness.'

Behind Mother's back, Bea raised her eyebrows.

What was it, we used to ask ourselves – that quality that she, we felt sure, misnamed. Was it courage? Was it strength, health, or high spirits? Something you could not give or take – a conundrum? A game of catch-as-catch-can?

'I know,' cried Bea. 'A sham!'

Whatever it was, we knew that Mother would let no wind of violence from within or without tear it from her. Although, one evening when Father High was with us, our astonished ears heard her proclaim that there might be a time when one had to slacken hold on it – let to – to catch at it again with a surer hand. In the way, we supposed, that the high-wire walker up among the painted stars of his canvas sky must wait to fling himself through the air until the bar he catches at has started to sway perversely from him. Oh no, no! That downward drag at our innards we could not bear, the belly swelling to the shape of a pear. Let happiness go by the board. 'After all, lots of people seem to make out without it,' Bea cried. It was too tricky a business. And might it not be that one had to be born with a flair for it?

'A flair would not be enough,' Mother answered. 'Take Father Hugh. He, if anyone, has a flair for it – a natural capacity! You've only to look at him when he's off guard, with you children, or helping me in the garden. But he rejects happiness! He casts it from him.'

'That is simply not true, Vera,' cried Father Hugh, overhearing her. 'It's just that I don't place an inordinate value on it like you. I don't think it's enough to carry one all the way. To the end, I mean – and after.'

'Oh, don't talk about the end when we're only in the middle,' cried Mother. And indeed, at that moment her own face shone with such happiness it was hard to believe that her earth was not her heaven. Certainly it was her constant contention that of happiness she had had a lion's share. This, however, we, in private, doubted. Perhaps there were times when she had had a surplus of it – when she was young, say, with her redoubtable father, whose love blazed circles around her, making winter into summer and ice into fire. Perhaps she did have a brimming measure in her early married years. By straining hard, we could find traces left in our minds from those days of milk and honey. Our father, while he lived, had cast a magic over everything, for us as well as for her. He held his love up over us like an umbrella and kept off the troubles that afterwards came down on us, pouring cats and dogs!

But if she did have more than the common lot of happiness in those early days, what use was that when we could remember so clearly how our father's death had ravaged her? And how could we forget the distress it brought on us when, afraid to let her out of our sight, Bea and I stumbled after her everywhere, through the woods and along the bank of the river, where, in the weeks that followed, she tried vainly to find peace.

The summer after Father died, we were invited to France to stay with friends, and when she went walking on the cliffs at Fécamp our fears for her grew frenzied, so that we hung on to

146

her arm and dragged at her skirt, hoping that like leaded weights we'd pin her down if she went too near the edge. But at night we had to abandon our watch, being forced to follow the conventions of a family still whole – a home still intact – and go to bed at the same time as the other children. It was at that hour, when the coast guard was gone from his rowing boat offshore and the sand was as cold and grey as the sea, that Mother liked to swim. And when she had washed, kissed, and left us, our hearts almost died inside us and we'd creep out of bed again to stand in our bare feet at the mansard and watch as she ran down the shingle, striking out when she reached the water where, far out, wave and sky and mist were one, and the greyness closed over her. If we took our eyes off her for an instant, it was impossible to find her again.

'Oh, make her turn back, God, please!' I prayed out loud one night.

Startled, Bea turned away from the window. 'She'll *have* to turn back sometime, won't she? Unless . . . ?'

Locking our damp hands together, we stared out again. 'She wouldn't!' I whispered. 'It would be a sin!'

Secure in the deterring power of sin, we let out our breath. Then Bea's breath caught again. 'What if she went out so far she used up all her strength? She couldn't swim back! It wouldn't be a sin, then!'

'It's the intention that counts,' I whispered.

A second later, we could see an arm lift heavily up and wearily cleave down, and at last Mother was in the shallows, wading back to shore.

'Don't let her see us!' cried Bea. As if our chattering teeth would not give us away when she looked in at us before she went to her own room on the other side of the corridor, where, later in the night, sometimes the sound of crying would reach us.

What was it worth – a happiness bought that dearly?

Mother had never questioned it. And once she told us, 'On a wintry day, I brought my own mother a snowdrop. It was the first one of the year – a bleak bud that had come up stunted before its time – and I meant it for a sign. But do you know what your grandmother said? "What good are snowdrops to me now?" Such a thing to say! What good is a snowdrop at all if it doesn't hold its value always, and never lose it! Isn't that the whole point of a snowdrop? And that is the whole point of happiness, too!

What good would it be if it could be erased without trace? Take me and those daffodils!' Stooping, she buried her face in a bunch that lay on the table waiting to be put in vases. 'If they didn't hold their beauty absolute and inviolable, do you think I could bear the sight of them after what happened when your father was in hospital?'

It was a fair question. When Father went to hospital, Mother went with him and stayed in a small hotel across the street so she could be with him all day from early to late. 'Because it was so awful for him – being in Dublin!' she said. 'You have no idea how he hated it.'

That he was dying neither of them realised. How could they know, as it rushed through the sky, that their star was a falling star! But one evening when she'd left him asleep Mother came home for a few hours to see how we were faring, and it broke her heart to see the daffodils out all over the place – in the woods, under the trees, and along the sides of the avenue. There had never been so many, and she thought how awful it was that Father was missing them. 'You sent up little bunches to him, you poor dears!' she said. 'Sweet little bunches, too – squeezed tight as posies by your little fists! But stuffed into vases they couldn't really make up to him for not being able to see them growing!'

So on the way back to the hospital she stopped her car and pulled a great bunch – the full of her arms. 'They took up the whole seat,' she said, 'and I was so excited at the thought of walking into his room and dumping them on his bed – you know – just plomping them so he could smell them, and feel them, and look and look! I didn't mean them to be put in vases, or anything ridiculous like that – it would have taken a rainwater barrel to hold them. Why, I could hardly see over them as I came up the steps; I kept tripping. But when I came into the hall, that nun – I told you about her – that nun came up to me, sprang out of nowhere it seemed, although I know now that she was waiting for me, knowing that somebody had to bring me to my senses. But the way she did it! Reached out and grabbed the flowers, letting lots of them fall – I remember them getting stood on. "Where are you going with those foolish flowers, you foolish woman?" she said. "Don't you know your husband is dying? Your prayers are all you can give him now!"

'She was right. I *was* foolish. But I wasn't cured. Afterwards, it was nothing but foolishness the way I dragged you children after me all over Europe. As if any one place was going to be different

148

from another, any better, any less desolate. But there was great satisfaction in bringing you places your father and I had planned to bring you – although in fairness to him I must say that he would not perhaps have brought you so young. And he would not have had an ulterior motive. But above all, he would not have attempted those trips in such a dilapidated car.'

Oh, that car! It was a battered and dilapidated red sports car, so depleted of accessories that when, eventually, we got a new car Mother still stuck out her hand on bends, and in wet weather jumped out to wipe the windscreen with her sleeve. And if fussed, she'd let down the window and shout at people, forgetting she now had a horn. How we had ever fitted into it all our luggage was a miracle.

'You were never lumpish – any of you!' Mother said proudly. 'But you were very healthy and very strong.' She turned to me. 'Think of how you got that car up the hill in Switzerland!'

'The Alps are not hills, Mother!' I pointed out coldly, as I had done at the time, when, as actually happened, the car failed to make it on one of the inclines. Mother let it run back until it wedged against the rock face, and I had to get out and push till she got going again in first gear. But when it got started it couldn't be stopped to pick me up until it got to the top, where they had to wait for me, and for a very long time.

'Ah, well,' she said, sighing wistfully at the thought of those trips. 'You got something out of them, I hope. All that travelling must have helped you with your geography and your history.'

We looked at each other and smiled, and then Mother herself laughed. 'Remember the time,' she said, 'when we were in Italy, and it was Easter, and all the shops were chock-full of food? The butchers' shops had poultry and game hanging up outside the doors fully feathered, and with their poor heads dripping blood, and in the windows they had poor little lambs and suckling pigs and young goats, all skinned and hanging by their hindfeet.' Mother shuddered. 'They think so much about food. I found it revolting. I had to hurry past. But Linda, who must have been only four then, dragged at me and stared and stared. You know how children are at that age; they have a morbid fascination for what is cruel and bloody. Her face was flushed and her eyes were wide. I hurried her back to the hotel. But next morning she crept into my room. She crept up to me and pressed against me. "Can't we go back, just once, and look again at that shop?" she whispered. "The shop where they have the little children hanging up for Easter!'' It was the young goats, of course, but I'd said "kids", I suppose. How we laughed.' But her face was grave. 'You were *so* good on those trips, all of you,' she said. 'You were really very good children in general. Otherwise I would never have put so much effort into rearing you, because I wasn't a bit maternal. You brought out the best in me! I put an unnatural effort into you, of course, because I was taking my standards from your father, forgetting that his might not have remained so inflexible if he had lived to middle age and was beset by life, like other parents.'

'Well, the job is nearly over now, Vera,' said Father Hugh. 'And you didn't do so badly.'

'That's right, Hugh,' said Mother, and she straightened up, and put her hand to her back the way she sometimes did in the garden when she got up from her knees after weeding. 'I didn't go over to the enemy anyway! We survived!' Then a flash of defiance came into her eyes. 'And we were happy. That's the main thing!'

Father Hugh frowned. 'There you go again!' he said.

Mother turned on him. 'I don't think you realise the onslaughts that were made upon our happiness! The minute Robert died, they came down on me – cohorts of relatives, friends, even strangers, all draped in black, opening their arms like bats to let me pass into their company. ''Life is a vale of tears,'' they said. ''You are privileged to find it out so young!'' Ugh! After I staggered onto my feet and began to take hold of life once more, they fell back defeated. And the first day I gave a laugh – pouff, they were blown out like candles. They weren't living in a real world at all; they belonged to a ghostly world where life was easy: all one had to do was sit and weep. It takes effort to push back the stone from the mouth of the tomb and walk out.'

Effort. Effort. Ah, but that strange-sounding word could invoke little sympathy from those who had not learned yet what it meant. Life must have been hardest for Mother in those years when we older ones were at college – no longer children, and still dependent on her. Indeed, we made more demands on her than ever then, having moved into new areas of activity and emotion. And our friends! Our friends came and went as freely as we did ourselves, so that the house was often like a café – and one where pets were not prohibited but took their places on our chairs and beds, as regardless as the people. And anyway it was hard to have sympathy for someone who got things into such a state as

Mother. All over the house there was clutter. Her study was like the returned-letter department of a post-office, with stacks of paper everywhere, bills paid and unpaid, letters answered and unanswered, tax returns, pamphelts, leaflets. If by mistake we left the door open on a windy day, we came back to find papers flapping through the air like frightened birds. Efficient only in that she managed eventually to conclude every task she began, it never seemed possible to outsiders that by Mother's methods anything whatever could be accomplished. In an attempt to keep order elsewhere, she made her own room the clearing house into which the rest of us put everything: things to be given away, things to be mended, things to be stored, things to be treasured, things to be returned – even things to be thrown out! By the end of the year, the room resembled an obsolescence dump. And no one could help her; the chaos of her life was as personal as an act of creation – one might as well try to finish another person's poem. As the years passed, Mother rushed around more hectically. And although Bea and I had married and were not at home any more, except at holiday time and for occasional week-ends, Linda was noisier than the two of us put together had been, and for every follower we had brought home she brought twenty. The house was never still. Now that we were reduced to being visitors, we watched Mother's tension mount to vertigo, knowing that, like a spinning top, she could not rest till she fell. But now at the smallest pretext Father Hugh would call in the doctor and Mother would be put on the mail boat and dispatched for London. For it was essential that she get far enough away to make phoning home every night prohibitively costly.

Unfortunately, the thought of departure often drove a spur into her and she redoubled her effort to achieve order in her affairs. She would be up until the early hours ransacking her desk. To her, as always, the shortest parting entailed a preparation as for death. And as if it were her end that was at hand, we would all be summoned, although she had no time to speak a word to us, because five minutes before departure she would still be attempting to reply to letters that were the acquisition of weeks and would have taken whole days to dispatch.

'Don't you know the taxi is at the door, Vera?' Father Hugh would say, running his hand through his grey hair and looking very dishevelled himself. She had him at times as distracted as herself. 'You can't do any more. You'll have to leave the rest till

151

you come back.'

'I can't, I can't!' Mother would cry. 'I'll have to cancel my plans.'

One day, Father Hugh opened the lid of her case, which was strapped up in the hall, and with a swipe of his arm he cleared all the papers on the top of the desk, pell-mell into the suitcase. 'You can sort them on the boat,' he said, 'or the train to London!'

Thereafter, Mother's luggage always included an empty case to hold the unfinished papers on her desk. And years afterwards a steward on the *Irish Mail* told us she was a familiar figure, working away at letters and bills nearly all the way from Holyhead to Euston. 'She gave it up about Rugby or Crewe,' he said. 'She'd get talking to someone in the compartment.' He smiled. 'There was one time coming down the train I was just in time to see her close up the window with a guilty look. I didn't say anything, but I think she'd emptied those papers of hers out the window!'

Quite likely. When we were children, even a few hours away from us gave her composure. And in two weeks or less, when she'd come home, the well of her spirit would be freshened. We'd hardly know her – her step so light, her eye so bright, and her love and patience once more freely flowing. But in no time at all the house would fill up once more with the noise and confusion of too many people and too many animals, and again we'd be fighting our corner with cats and dogs, bats, mice, bees and even wasps. 'Don't kill it!' Mother would cry if we raised a hand to an angry wasp. 'Just catch it, dear, and put it outside. Open the window and let it fly away!' But even this treatment could at times be deemed too harsh. 'Wait a minute. Close the window!' she'd cry. 'It's too cold outside. It will die. That's why it came in, I suppose! Oh dear, what will we do?' Life would be going full blast again.

There was only one place Mother found rest. When she was at breaking point and fit to fall, she'd go out into the garden – not to sit or stroll around but to dig, to drag up weeds, to move great clumps of corms or rhizomes, or indeed quite frequently to haul huge rocks from one place to another. She was always laying down a path, building a dry wall, or making compost heaps as high as hills. However jaded she might be going out, when dark forced her in at last her step had the spring of a daisy. So if she did not succeed in defining happiness to our understanding, we could see that, whatever it was, she possessed it to the full when she was in her garden.

One of us said as much one Sunday when Bea and I had dropped round for the afternoon. Father Hugh was with us again. 'It's an unthinking happiness, though,' he cavilled. We were standing at the drawing-room window, looking out to where in the fading light we could see Mother on her knees weeding, in the long border that stretched from the house right down to the woods. 'I wonder how she'd take it if she were stricken down and had to give up that heavy work!' he said. Was he perhaps a little jealous of how she could stoop and bend? He himself had begun to use a stick. I was often a little jealous of her myself, because although I was married and had children of my own, I had married young and felt the weight of living as heavy as a weight of years. 'She doesn't take care of herself,' Father Hugh said sadly. 'Look at her out there with nothing under her knees to protect her from the damp ground.' It was almost too dim for us to see her, but even in the drawing room it was chilly. 'She should not be let stay out there after the sun goes down.'

'Just you try to get her in then!' said Linda, who had come into the room in time to hear him. 'Don't you know by now anyway that what will kill another person only seems to make Mother thrive?'

Father Hugh shook his head again. 'You seem to forget it's not younger she's getting!' He fidgeted and fussed, and several times went to the window to stare our apprehensively. He was really getting quite elderly.

'Come and sit down, Father Hugh,' Bea said, and to take his mind off Mother she turned on the light and blotted out the garden. Instead of seeing through the window, we saw into it as into a mirror, and there between the flower-laden tables and the lamps it was ourselves we saw moving vaguely. Like Father Hugh, we, too, were waiting for her to come in before we called an end to the day.

'Oh, this is ridiculous!' Father Hugh cried at last. 'She'll have to listen to reason.' And going back to the window he threw it open. 'Vera!' he called. 'Vera!' – sternly, so sternly that, more intimate than an endearment, his tone shocked us. 'She didn't hear me,' he said, turning back blinking at us in the lighted room. 'I'm going to her.' And in a minute he was gone from the room. As he ran down the garden path, we stared at each other, astonished; his step, like his voice, was the step of a lover. 'I'm coming, Vera!' he cried.

Although she was never stubborn except in things that

153

mattered, Mother had not moved. In the wholehearted way she did everything, she was bent down close to the ground. It wasn't the light only that was dimming; her eyesight also was failing, I thought, as instinctively I followed Father Hugh.

But halfway down the path I stopped. I had seen something he had not: Mother's hand that appeared to support itself in a forked branch of an old tree peony she had planted as a bride was not in fact gripping it but impaled upon it. And the hand that appeared to be grubbing in the clay in fact was sunk into the soft mould. 'Mother!' I screamed, and I ran forward, but when I reached her I covered my face with my hands. 'Oh Father Hugh!' I cried. 'Is she dead?'

It was Bea who answered, hysterical. 'She is! She is!' she cried, and she began to pound Father Hugh on the back with her fists, as if his pessimistic words had made this happen.

But Mother was not dead. And at first the doctor even offered hope of her pulling through. But from the moment Father Hugh lifted her up to carry her into the house we ourselves had no hope, seeing how effortlessly he, who was not strong, could carry her. When he put her down on her bed, her head hardly creased the pillow. Mother lived for four more hours.

Like the days of her life, those four hours that Mother lived were packed tight with concern and anxiety. Partly conscious, party delirious, she seemed to think the counterpane was her desk, and she scrabbled her fingers upon it as if trying to sort out a muddle of bills and correspondence. No longer indifferent now, we listened, anguished, to the distracted cries that had for all our lifetime been so familiar to us. 'Oh, where is it? Where is it? I had it a minute ago! Where on earth did I put it?'

'Vera, Vera, stop worrying,' Father Hugh pleaded, but she waved him away and went on sifting through the sheets as if they were sheets of paper. 'Oh, Vera!' he begged. 'Listen to me. Do you not know – '

Bea pushed between them. 'You're not to tell her!' she commanded. 'Why frighten her?'

'But it ought not to frighten her,' said Father Hugh. 'This is what I was always afraid would happen – that she'd be frightened when it came to the end.'

At that moment, as if to vindicate him, Mother's hands fell idle on the coverlet, palms upward and empty. And turning her head she stared at each of us in turn, beseechingly. 'I cannot face it,' she whispered. 'I can't! I can't! I can't!'

'Oh, my God!' Bea said, and she started to cry.

'Vera. For God's sake listen to me,' Father Hugh cried, and pressing his face to hers, as close as a kiss, he kept whispering to her, trying to cast into the dark tunnel before her the light of his faith.

But it seemed to us that Mother must already be looking into God's exigent eyes. 'I can't!' she cried. 'I can't!'

Then her mind came back from the stark world of the spirit to the world where her body was still detained, but even that world was now a whirling kaleidoscope of things which only she could see. Suddenly her eyes focussed, and, catching at Father Hugh, she pulled herself up a little and pointed to something we could not see. 'What will be done with them?' Her voice was anxious. 'They ought to be put in water anyway,' she said, and, leaning over the edge of the bed, she pointed to the floor. 'Don't step on that one!' she said sharply. Then, more sharply still, she addressed us all. 'Have them sent to the public ward,' she said peremptorily. 'Don't let that nun take them; she'll only put them on the altar. And God doesn't want them! He made them for *us* – not for Himself!'

It was the familiar rhetoric that all her life had characterised her utterances. For a moment we were mystified. Then Bea gasped. 'The daffodils!' she cried. 'The day Father died!' And over her face came the light that had so often blazed over Mother's. Leaning across the bed, she pushed Father Hugh aside. And, putting out her hands, she held Mother's face between her palms as tenderly as if it were the face of a child. 'It's all right, Mother. You don't *have* to face it! It's over!' Then she who had so fiercely forbade Father Hugh to do so blurted out the truth. 'You've finished with this world, Mother,' she said, and confident that her tidings were joyous, her voice was strong.

Mother made the last effort of her life and grasped at Bea's meaning. She let out a sigh, and, closing her eyes, she sank back, and this time her head sank so deep into the pillow that it would have been dented had it been a pillow of stone.

Biographical Notes

GEORGE MOORE (1852-1933): Born in Co. Mayo, the son of a wealthy, landowning M.P., he went to Paris in 1873 to paint but failing as an artist, returned to Ireland in 1879. He was associated with Yeats and Lady Gregory in the founding of the Abbey Theatre, wrote three volumes of short stories, many novels and a celebrated autobiography, *Hail and Farewell*. Lived in London from 1911 until his death.

E. Œ SOMERVILLE (1858-1949) and MARTIN ROSS (1862-1915): Edith Somerville was born in Corfu where her father was stationed, but the following year she was brought home to the family seat in Co. Cork where she spent most of her life. Violet Martin, her cousin, was born in Co. Galway, and they first met in 1886. The literary partnership commenced with *An Irish Cousin* in 1889 and three celebrated collections of *IRISH R.M.* (Resident Magistrate) stories were published in 1899, 1908 and 1915. Violet Martin died in 1915 but Edith Somerville, believing that death had not ended their collaboration, continued to publish all her subsequent writings under their joint names.

LYNN DOYLE (1873-1961): Born in Co. Down, he started as a bank clerk in Belfast at the age of 16 and was a bank manager in Co. Dublin when he retired in 1934. A prolific novelist, poet and playwright, he is most famous for his many volumes of short stories about the mythical Northern Ireland border village of Ballygullion, the first of which was published in 1908 and the last in 1957.

SEAMUS O'KELLY (1875-1918): Born in Co. Galway, he worked as a journalist in Ireland before moving to the *Saturday Evening Post* in New York in 1912. For health reasons he returned to Ireland in 1915 and in May, 1918, died of a heart attack after the offices of a political paper he was editing were raided by British forces. His plays were performed in the Abbey Theatre and in London and he wrote two novels and some half-dozen collections of short stories, *The Rector* being from the second of these, *Waysiders,* published in 1918.

DANIEL CORKERY (1878-1964): Born in Cork, he was an important influence on many Irish writers, notably Sean O'Faolain and Frank O'Connor. Professor of English at University College, Cork from 1931-1947, his own work was intensely nationalistic and in the latter part of his life he abandoned English as a means of literary expression. *Joy* is from *A Munster Twilight,* the first of his four volumes of short stories, published in 1916.

JAMES STEPHENS (1880-1950): Born in Dublin, he lived in London from 1924 until his death. His best known work is his novel *The Crock of Gold* (1912) which won him an international reputation, but he also published a number of poetry collections and two volumes of short stories, *Here Are Ladies* (1913) and *Etched in Moonlight* (1928) from the latter of which *Desire* is taken.

JAMES JOYCE (1882-1941): Generally regarded as the most important and influential English-language prose writer of the twentieth century. Apart from some poems and a play, he wrote one collection of stories, *Dubliners* (1914), and three novels, *A Portrait of the Artist as a Young Man* (1916), *Ulysses* (1922) and *Finnegan's Wake* (1939). From 1904 until his death he lived abroad, mostly in Zürich and Paris. His last visit to Dublin was in 1912.

LIAM O'FLAHERTY (1897-   ): Born in the Aran Islands, he is one of the giants of the Irish short story. Apart from stories, he wrote many novels and three autobiographical books. He served in the British Army in the First World War and then fought in the Irish Revolution. He spent many years in the U.S., but has lived mainly in Dublin since 1946.

ELIZABETH BOWEN (1899-1973): Born in Dublin, her family home was Bowen's Court, Co. Cork. She divided her time mostly between London and Ireland, and her international reputation as a writer is based on a succession of distinguished novels and short stories.

SEAN O'FAOLAIN (1900-   ): Born in Cork, he fought on the Republican side in the Irish Civil War. Probably the most distinguished all-round man of letters in the Irish cultural scene since Yeats. Playwright, novelist, poet, translator, essayist, biographer, and editor, he is best known as a short story writer with seven collections to his name. *The Kitchen* is from *The Talking Trees* (1971).

FRANK O'CONNOR (1903-1966): Born in Cork. Largely self-educated, he worked as a librarian until 1938 and thereafter devoted all his time to writing. His first collection of stories, *Guests of the Nation,* was published in 1931. Among his other books are some half-dozen further short story collections, two novels, many translations from Irish poetry, biography, two volumes of autobiography, criticism, and a book on Shakespeare. He was a Director of the Abbey Theatre (where he had two plays produced) from 1936-39 and a brilliantly persuasive lecturer and broadcaster.

PATRICK BOYLE (1905-   ): Born in Co. Antrim, a retired bank manager, he has written one novel and three collections of short stories. *At Night All Cats Are Grey* is the title story of his first collection, published in 1966.

MICHAEL McLAVERTY (1907-   ): One of Northern Ireland's most distinguished writers, he spent most of his life teaching in Belfast where he now lives in retirement. He wrote eight novels and many short stories.

BRYAN MacMAHON (1909-   ): Born in Co. Kerry where he taught for most of his life. He has written two volumes of short stories, novels, plays and pageants, and has also been active in the field of translating from the Irish.

ANTHONY C. WEST (1910-   ): One of the most neglected of Northern Ireland's writers, he has published one volume of short stories, *River's End* (1960), and some half-dozen novels. He lived for many years in Wales and is now living in London.

MARY LAVIN (1912-   ): Born in the U.S.A. but came to Ireland as a child and was educated at University College, Dublin. She has written two novels but her world-wide reputation rests firmly on her short stories, ten collections of which have so far appeared. *Happiness* dates from 1969.

NEL BESTSELLERS

T 51277	'THE NUMBER OF THE BEAST'	*Robert Heinlein*	£2.25
T 51382	FAIR WARNING	*Simpson & Burger*	£1.75
T 50246	TOP OF THE HILL	*Irwin Shaw*	£1.95
T 46443	FALSE FLAGS	*Noel Hynd*	£1.25
T 49272	THE CELLAR	*Richard Laymen*	£1.25
T 45692	THE BLACK HOLE	*Alan Dean Foster*	95p
T 49817	MEMORIES OF ANOTHER DAY	*Harold Robbins*	£1.95
T 53231	THE DARK	*James Herbert*	£1.50
T 45528	THE STAND	*Stephen King*	£1.75
T 50203	IN THE TEETH OF THE EVIDENCE	*Dorothy L. Sayers*	£1.25
T 50777	STRANGER IN A STRANGE LAND	*Robert Heinlein*	£1.75
T 50807	79 PARK AVENUE	*Harold Robbins*	£1.75
T 51722	DUNE	*Frank Herbert*	£1.75
T 50149	THE INHERITORS	*Harold Robbins*	£1.75
T 49620	RICH MAN, POOR MAN	*Irwin Shaw*	£1.60
T 46710	EDGE 36: TOWN ON TRIAL	*George G. Gilman*	£1.00
T 51552	DEVIL'S GUARD	*Robert Elford*	£1.50
T 53296	THE RATS	*James Herbert*	£1.50
T 50874	CARRIE	*Stephen King*	£1.50
T 43245	THE FOG	*James Herbert*	£1.50
T 52575	THE MIXED BLESSING	*Helen Van Slyke*	£1.75
T 38629	THIN AIR	*Simpson & Burger*	95p
T 38602	THE APOCALYPSE	*Jeffrey Konvitz*	95p
T 46796	NOVEMBER MAN	*Bill Granger*	£1.25

NEL P.O. BOX 11, FALMOUTH TR10 9EN, CORNWALL

Postage charge:

U.K. Customers. Please allow 40p for the first book, 18p for the second book, 13p for each additional book ordered, to a maximum charge of £1.49, in addition to cover price.

B.F.P.O. & Eire. Please allow 40p for the first book, 18p for the second book, 13p per copy for the next 7 books, thereafter 7p per book, in addition to cover price.

Overseas Customers. Please allow 60p for the first book plus 18p per copy for each additional book, in addition to cover price.

Please send cheque or postal order (no currency).

Name ....

Address ....

....

Title ....

While every effort is made to keep prices steady, it is sometimes necessary to increase prices at short notice. New English Library reserve the right to show on covers and charge new retail prices which may differ from those advertised in the text or elsewhere.(6)